M000159255

THE CARNIVOROUS PLANT

ANDREA MAYO
THE CARNIVOROUS PLANT

Translated from Catalan by
Laura McGloughlin

3TimesRebel

First published by 3TimesRebel Press in 2022, our first year of existence.

Title: *The Carnivorous Plant* by Andrea Mayo

Original title: *La Planta Carnívora* © Flavia Company, 2021
c/o Ute Körner Literary Agent

Originally published by Raval Edicions, SLU, Proa

Translation from Catalan: Copyright © Laura McGloughlin, 2022

Design and layout: Enric Jardí

Illustrations: Anna Pont Armengol

Editing and proof reading: Greg Mulhern, Carme Bou, Bibiana Mas

Maria-Mercè Marçal's poem *Deriva*:
© heiresses of Maria-Mercè Marçal

Translation of Maria-Mercè Marçal's poem *Deriva*:
© Dr Sam Abrams

The translation of this book is supported by Institut Ramon Llull

LLLL institut ramon llull

Printed and bound by TJ Books, Padstow, Cornwall, England
Paperback ISBN: 978-1-7398236-3-4
eBook ISBN: 978-1-7398236-6-5
978-1-7391287-2-2

www.3timesrebel.com

'It's difficult to write about the living, because they are persons that keep on changing.'

The Lost Letter of Andrea Mayo,
Flavia Company

1

FROM NOW ON I'LL TELL THE WHOLE TRUTH. FROM NOW ON everything I say will be true. You'll say, I don't believe it.

How easy it would be not to swallow the horror, or think it could only happen to others.

That wouldn't happen to me.

I wouldn't stand for it.

How could you allow someone to do such a thing to you.

I used to be amongst you before, in the club that scorns the weak. The one that considers they are to blame. Complicit.

What is weakness?

And why tell the truth now? Why not before?

You haven't the slightest idea what it's like, the fear of someone persecuting you. You haven't had to change your name, country, language. You are not me, even though I used to be one of you.

What does a carnivorous plant have that others lack?

Think about it.

More showy.

Harder to cultivate.

Think about it.

The carnivorous plant has its own way of moving. It swallows. It traps live prey. The trap is activated when they make contact with it. And if they are within reach for long enough then it shuts them up inside itself.

You won't come out alive if you get close to her.

No one has got close to her for years.

It makes her inaccessible.

What's she called?

Ibana.

Like iguana.

My sister introduced her to me. She'd warned me: she's a little strange, but interesting to talk to.

I don't know, she makes me feel lazy, I confessed to her afterwards. She thinks a lot of herself. She thinks she's beyond good and evil. She doesn't drink, she doesn't smoke, she doesn't fuck. She's scary.

But interesting to talk to.

What does she talk about?

What shit do people who seem interesting talk about? That was a clue, but I didn't know how to see it. The people who seem interesting talk about the people they consider interesting with the sole objective of seeming interesting to them.

People love being the topic of conversation.

They make themselves experts on you. All of a sudden you are their subject.

But what happens to you.

But what I've noticed you do.

But what an authentic life you lead.

But are you a Taurus?

But you have a real gift for this.

But this and that.

They watch you. They say all this to you. They make you fall at their feet. Or rather, on their petals.

Come a little closer.

Carnivorous plants have no scent. Who would dare to smell them? So they don't need one. The law of least resistance. They have safeguards against wasting energy in case the trapped prey has no nutritional value.

And what's her name?

I already told you.

You're right, Ibana. I'd forgotten. Your friendly iguana, so still until the source of energy she needs appears.

And what did she chat about?

She talked about the evil in the world.

She has a little iguana. The iguaneenie. She is a sliver of flesh that remained of a male victim who escaped her. No one knows how he managed to get away. Some say he received outside help.

1

I'VE ALWAYS BEEN SEDUCTIVE. IT WAS BUILT-IN, THE EFFECT I'VE had on women since my youth. All ages, all classes, all civil states, all sexual tendencies.

A hand gesture, a wink, a poem recited off the cuff or a story in which they are the star. Not other skills, but definitely this one. And the iguana couldn't be less skilled.

You touched me, you're staying, she sentenced me.

What do you mean I'm staying?

Ancient times. It sounded like a speech from ancient times.

I'm not like other women. You touched me, you're staying with me.

As if she was defending a kind of overdeveloped virginity.

You've stained me, you must pay.

And the time you take to react is enough for the mechanism to click silently into motion.

1

SHE HIT ME SO HARD A GASH OPENED UP CLOSE TO THE TEAR duct of my left eye and began to bleed.

Not only did she not apologise, she walked out after slamming a door. A car door. We were in a shitty town in a shitty place, in the middle of nowhere.

I called her mobile non-stop for a long time and she didn't pick up. Nor would she. She always did this.

I took a photo of my wound, my bloodied face. I sent it to her via WhatsApp.

She answered: I've maimed you.

I asked her to come with me to A & E.

No, I've maimed you.

Then take me there.

No.

I drove myself for over an hour without stopping. The wound was burning. The collar of my shirt was bloodstained. Droplets, red on white.

At the hospital I was told: You must report this. The nurse looked at my eye first and then at the droplets of blood on my clothes and then the car keys in my hand and then my hands which must have betrayed my nerves. Perhaps in their non-verbal language they were making the movements everyone's hands make when they're pretending.

I realised all this because I answered, No, I was on my own, I did it with my bag, I don't even know how. I kept looking at the bag as if it wasn't mine, with an expression of how the hell did you do this to me, what part of you cuts.

They believed me because how could they not believe me. That is, they didn't believe me but how could they have told me so. I don't look like an abused woman.

Fool! What do abused people look like?

They don't look any different, that's a prejudiced view. They don't look like anything in particular. They're not all the same. The disaster is within and those seeking to swallow them know the signs well.

1

HOW DID YOU KNOW THAT YOU HAD TO GET AWAY?

When I started to be afraid of her.

And when was that?

When I realised that she was never distressed by mistreating me.

Every night I'd get into bed beside her and think: I can't die this way, here, with this person nearby. I can't end my life with someone who unmoved would leave me to die.

Are you aware your speech is very disjointed?

Following a train of thought while narrating so much horror is impossible.

What would you say your predominant state of mind was?

I lived on high alert. I didn't know what I could say or do; not at all. Anything and everything was susceptible to irritating her and provoking one of her fits of rage. Silence, too. But not always the same things. She gave no clues. That's terror, isn't it?

1

SHE INSULTED ME. SHE SCORNED EVERY STEP I'D TAKEN. AND those I was taking.

Those people who say they love you don't love you. Can't you see that they don't love you? Bit by bit the plant establishes her roots where you have yours, which are destroyed little by little. There comes a time when only her circle, her friendships, are worthwhile, and you distance yourself from your own, from your family, from everything, so as not to hear it any more, so she doesn't hurt you any more, so she might be quiet, please. I was overwhelmed by her shouting. I needed silence. To move and have nothing happen. To speak and not unleash a storm.

You do everything possible to avoid suffocating yet the only thing you achieve is to move deeper into the funnel. You don't have time to catch your breath. In the end you don't even have time to catch your breath.

1

A JAPANESE RESTAURANT. A CELEBRATION. NOT EVEN A QUARTER of an hour had passed since we sat down on the tatami.

She came out with, You like tall women.

I already knew I was lost, that every comment and every answer, even saying nothing, would be a mistake.

I put one of those fat makis in my mouth. A California roll. I stared at the black tray they'd been served on. There were three left. I stayed quiet.

You like tall women, she repeated. The iguana, who was shorter than what she considered to be tall, said it again.

I shrugged my shoulders and as I chewed with both sides of my mouth full I shook my head and after swallowing half the maki and almost choking, I said no, I like you. Then I went about sweeping my tongue over the food stuck in my teeth and gums.

I'm not tall.

Exactly.

But you like tall women.

No, not at all.

If you didn't like tall women you wouldn't have been with her.

Here we go again. I let my eyes fall on the delicate wine-coloured flowers painted on the paper decorating the walls of the private dining room. A crane with outstretched wings. A desire to escape to Japan. Far away. I sighed trying to disguise it as a cough.

Are you sighing?

No, of course not.

She hated all my exes and the last one, who was tall, more than anyone else.

I felt a chunk of rice with salmon and avocado in my oesophagus. And I saw how the filaments between her petals were closing around me, little by little. I had to move quickly to get out of there, but I knew very well that if she sensed the slightest movement of intent to escape, she would crush me forever.

I don't like tall women, Iba.

You see? You always say she wasn't so important to you, but see how you must have liked her; not to mind her being tall if, as you say, you hate, are disgusted by tall women. How she must have turned you on for you to move in with her.

I didn't say I hated them. Tall women.

You always lie. Look what's happened to you, from having lied so much. Your life is a mess. And you know why? Because you're a bitch, that's what you are.

Then she got up and left me sitting there on the floor, three California rolls and a well-chilled bottle of white, still half-full, in front of me. She left me there with the dinner to which she'd invited me and that of course in her untimely exit she'd left unpaid.

So I continued to sit there, knocking back more wine than food, feeling suffocated but looking for my phone and calling her begging forgiveness, please, I want us to be okay, what's the point of all this. But as usual she didn't pick up and as usual I didn't know whether she'd been knocked down by a car or if she'd taken a taxi home, to a Y-shaped house which I wanted to live in less and less. Who dares to go there and who dares not to go there; prepare yourself for either.

Pray if she wakes up and you're not there. Pray if she wakes up and you are there.

Now I ask myself, what the hell was I so scared of?

She convinced me she was willing to destroy me. Because she was like that. And she was on the verge of succeeding. So many times.

1

THANKS FOR THINKING OF ME. THAT WAS HOW I RESPONDED TO a birthday message I got on WhatsApp.

Who was it?

No good could come of that question. I wished no one had messaged me, no one had remembered my birthday, the way no one remembered hers. It didn't occur to the iguaneenie to give her a present.

Carme.

The one you fucked once?

She was referring to a time long before I knew her, long before there was anything between us, Ibana and I. My sexual and romantic history drove her up the wall.

I was silent thinking, Twice, it was twice, and if someday she finds out she'll be upset, but if I tell her it was twice now the fallout will be fatal. Two and a half times, to be exact. Fatal.

Yes.

And why did you answer her?

I just said thank you.

What did you say?

Thanks for thinking of me.

So you didn't tell her you're with me.

If you want I'll text her again.

It's not about whether you text her again, it's about the fact you always act as if I don't exist. We're in Thailand together and you answer her as if you're on your own.

I don't answer as if I'm on my own, I said while feeling how alone I was.

Oh, no? You never remember to think in plural. And anyway, why did you go to bed with her? She's a despicable slag.

Maybe, I agreed as I thought, All the women I've gone to bed with seem shitty to you. And I felt like laughing and blurting out, I fucked her because she wasn't tall. But who'd have dared.

Maybe, you say?

Definitely, I said.

You're lying. You always lie. And you know why? Because your whole life is a lie, that's why. Because you're a fraud.

She put on her shoes, took a few steps, raised her hand, stopped a tuk-tuk and disappeared. I stayed there in front of the guy massaging my feet, still, rooted to the seat, wilting under the glance of commiseration the masseur was trying to hide, my heart in my mouth, with a pain that was so all-consuming I didn't have the strength to disguise it as irritation.

1

BUT WHEN DID IT START?

I can't be sure. It was there from the beginning. The question is when did I realise. The red flags were there. I threw white paint at them so they turned pink.

You can't ask yourself how you fall into a trap. They're designed for that to occur. Disguised in the earth, in the trees, in life itself. You happen to pass by and they spring into action, they move quickly, they make a dry click after which you know something isn't right. A well, a net, a snare. Were you not walking carefully enough? I'm trusting. Are clever people wary? Are wary people selfish? Selfish people only fall into their own traps, not those set by others.

When I looked around I was already trapped and no one could hear me. I shouted the lie that everything was fine so loudly it was impossible to hear the shoves, the slaps, the insults, the slamming doors.

Don't look at me like that. What you want is to understand and that's impossible. You want to understand because you think there'll be an explanation. And the worst thing of all is you think you'll find it in me.

What did I do so wrong that someone would treat me that way and I wouldn't flee instantly?

You don't ask how it's possible to abuse someone. You ask how it's possible to endure it.

Barabbas was saved because he was relatable. People identified with him.

You know how easy it is to walk down stairs, let's say fourteen or fifteen floors, and how difficult it is to walk back up?

Listen to what I'm telling you: wanting to understand is one of the most powerful reasons for falling into the trap. Accepting that you can't is the door that must be opened to escape.

I won't explain the why to you here. But just in case, the how.

1

WE SHOULD GO TO THERAPY, I SUGGESTED.

You should go, she answered.

Shall we both go?

She agreed because deep down she was confused by so much unhappiness. She didn't have a good relationship with her family or any of her exes, not even with her daughter.

I left feeling happy after the first session. Or should I say hopeful. Maybe there was a road towards healing, of opening a line of communication. I asked her, how was it for you.

We're not going back. You were clearly trying to seduce her and she played along with your game. She's fascinated by you. She'll agree with everything you say. You knew each other beforehand, didn't you?

How can something like that occur to you?

I'm not an idiot, Andrea. You're disgusting.

And after speeding up she raised a hand and got into a taxi and I immediately rang her mobile to beg her for a truce, a break please, please, a little peace, but of course she didn't answer so there I stayed, in the middle of the street, wanting to bash my head against the nearest wall.

Such malice seemed unthinkable to me. Within me — a lifeline — there was the sudden sound of invisible songs from unknown lands waiting for me to grasp the beauty of life in my hands once again. I have never travelled so far in time and space as I did in those moments.

CRUELTY

THE FILM BEGINS. A MAN DEEP IN THOUGHT IS WALKING cross-country. He's tall, strong, rather young. With every step his boots sink a little into the ground. Suddenly the camera focuses on a nest falling from a tree. It zooms in, close up; there are three chicks. They attract the strong man's eyes. He leaves his path, picks up the nest in those rough lumberjack or farmer hands, carefully places it inside his shirt, touching his chest, climbs easily up the trunk and deposits the nest on a wide and sturdy branch with the utmost care.

He climbs down from the tree and heaves a sigh, even brushes off a few pieces of bark that have stuck to his clothes and resumes walking.

He comes to a cabin in the middle of nowhere.

The camera enters the dwelling before him and finds two thin boys of seven or eight, hidden in an eyes-squeezed-shut silence, under the bed. They are holding hands.

Off camera the strong man's footsteps on the wooden floor can be heard. The man looks in some buckets. Empty. He is visibly angered by them. He raises his eyebrows. He takes off his belt. He walks towards the bed. He pulls one of the kids by the arm. They are clinging so tightly to one another that both are dragged out.

When he has hauled them out, he begins to beat them with the belt. Then he sets about kicking them. One of the boys receives a kick to his head. The man's boots are hard. The boy starts bleeding. The other one tries to help him. His hands are so small he can't seem to stanch the blood. He takes off his t-shirt, but it's not long before it's as red as his hands. The strong man grabs the knife from the sheath in which he carries it strapped to his back and with a single flick he cuts the jugular vein of the boy who was no doubt already dead, in front of the helpless eyes of the one who tried in vain to save him.

1

HAVE YOU EVER LOVED SOMEONE WHO DIDN'T LOVE themselves? Have you ever had the feeling you could save someone from desperation and darkness? Haven't you ever believed that love conquers all? Aren't you one of those people whose heart breaks when they see an injured animal trying to survive?

The worst thing that can happen to a carnivore is not wanting to be a carnivore and thinking they aren't one and insisting they aren't one and not recognising that their acts are the work of what they are and not what they want to be.

She was a bottomless well. Even though I'd thrown my heart at her, she continued telling me, after chewing without even tasting it, The thing is that you don't love me. You don't love me. You don't love me. What a refrain. And of course I loved her, but as the therapist finally told me, it's her or you. Either her or you.

There are so many wars within what's called love, aren't there?

The first time we met up was to go to the theatre. The play? Doubt. What a sign. Doubt. The constructive force of faith and the destructive force of defamation. Counter-accusations.

Rain was forecast and she was carrying a very big red umbrella. When we came out onto the street, not a single drop was falling, but I asked her to open it. It was an excuse to walk in each other's embrace. We stayed up until the small hours. And no, I didn't sense disaster that night. Precisely for that reason I invited her into my bed. And precisely because I didn't sense disaster she accepted. She made it clear she hadn't been with anyone for years. I should have read that as a sign of mortal danger. She was a firearm. Loaded. I was the ideal target.

1

THE TRUTH IS I'M NOT HUNGRY.

Film evenings in front of the fire. She didn't let me read. You're absent when you're reading, she'd say. So cinema it was. My stomach was in knots, with no desire for dinner. I remember my fear when expressing my lack of appetite. I remember my fear.

I don't know, maybe I ate too much lunch.

So I have to eat dinner alone, you won't eat anything because you don't want it and we can't have a normal peaceful Sunday evening because the princess says she doesn't fancy having dinner.

But I'm here anyway, with you, by your side.

You're doing it to piss me off.

Please, Ibana, let's not start, let me breathe.

Let you breathe? Watch how I let you breathe right now. You can keep all your shitty air.

Lettuce on the floor, tomatoes swimming across the tiles, oil splashed everywhere, one sad pepper stuck against the stucco on the wall, some trembling radishes in a corner.

She put on a jacket, eyes spitting fire as she insulted me.

You're a piece of shit, a motherfucker, that's what you are; let me breathe, she says, and how I'll let you breathe, no one has to ask me for air, who d'you think you are?

But I was just saying.

You're always just saying. You're a bad person, Andrea, you're violent.

Violent how?

What you do is called passive violence. Read up on it. That's what it is, you hypocrite. The thing is you won't have dinner and you ask me to leave so you can breathe. And that's what I'm doing, obeying you, see? I'm going, you asshole, that's what you are, I can't relax around you, you're a sadist, that's what you are.

She packed a suitcase with some of her things and left. In time I came to realise this was a strategy her father used to use, too: abuse and leave immediately .

In the middle of a winter's night she started walking along a dark road, and covered the five kilometres from the house where we were to the nearest hotel. Or so I supposed, because she'd done it so many other times for similar reasons. So I thought, because of course however many times I called her mobile she didn't answer and however many times I went out searching I didn't find her.

1

AFTERWARDS SHE'D WANT TO FUCK. AND I'D NOT WANT TO EVEN kiss her. So many insults and shoves and hair-pulling and slaps. So much fear. So much contempt.

She started to check whether I was wet when I got into bed. At night she'd touch my cunt as soon as I lay down, just to know.

You're not wet. You're dry. You don't love me. You've never loved me. You don't love me, that's for sure.

Then tell me why am I with you? If I don't love you, leave me.

A blow wherever she reached first. Or a kick. And then leaving the bed. Leaving home. Not returning all night.

It reached a point where I'd even want her to get angry and storm out. Just to leave me alone. To be able to sleep. Not having to have her lying on my body. 'You're weighing on me a bit', in the middle of the night, suffocating. 'See? You don't love me any more.' To be left alone. Maybe even masturbate. Sometimes thinking about her, what utter lunacy. For how much I'd loved her, for how much I could have loved her and would now be impossible. Every day was more difficult. I couldn't die by her side, but I didn't know how to leave her either. She did, she left me again and again, she'd say, this is over. She'd say it after clouting me and insulting me and ridiculing me. 'This is over.' That was her trick. Then I'd go after her and say, No, what do you mean it's over, we can make it, we could be happy, why can't you just believe that I love you? But a carnivorous plant doesn't need to be loved, but feared.

So every night before getting into bed I'd go to the toilet, spit on my hand a few times and thoroughly wet my cunt. To save myself the shouts, save myself the insults, save my life, dead inside, but wet.

1

YOU WERE FAKING. YOU DIDN'T COME. YOU'RE LYING TO ME, AS usual.

It was impossible not to deceive her. It had to begin one day or another. I knew very well her daughter was living a lie, the poor thing, saying she was going to university but skipping all her classes, claiming she'd passed subjects she hadn't even attended. I felt so sorry for her, tall and thin and pretty but twisted and fearful. Who could survive those fits of rage. Imitating those of Ibana's father, who had beaten them — her and her sisters — to the point of terrorising them. It seems he left one of them simple-minded. And made her into a carnivore.

Of course from time to time I defended myself. Once, while she was beating me, I shoved her off me and she fell down the stairs. I thought, now she'll die and keep on destroying my life, yet at the same time, I felt a primal sense of relief. No one will believe she committed suicide. Easier to think she slipped and fell. A perfect explanation.

She stayed alive. So whole. Always alert, even while she was sleeping. If I was agitated in my sleep, she'd wake up then wake me to ask, what were you dreaming, about who, what are you hiding from me.

You didn't come, you were faking your orgasm.

It was a little one, I'd say.

Then she'd put her hand on my cunt, Stop lying, you're not even wet, you've fucked so much in your life you can't do it any more.

I felt like first throwing up then replying, I can't bear you, I just can't any more, what are you a holy virgin who's only fucked those who got close to you, those poor things who risked their lives, how I envy your ex-husband and your ex-lovers, all free, how the fuck did they get out of here, how did they do it.

It was a little one, I don't know, maybe I'm tired.

I felt like dying right there.

1

BEFORE I MARRIED HER — YOU TOUCHED ME, YOU'RE MARRYING me — a friend, also a painter, called me. Robin called me and told me, I know from a reliable source that she swallows her companions, she's a praying mantis — so he said and I laughed. I replied, how do you know? I can't tell you. Oh, the usual anonymous comment — mind your own business, Rob. But I'm telling you in all seriousness. I know for sure she eats people who go to bed with her, she pulls out their intestines and ties them around their necks and strangles them, she starves their brains of oxygen, she keeps the brains for herself and then swallows them whole, little by little, as if she were the snake in *The Little Prince*, you remember that drawing, don't you. I didn't let him finish, I thought, what's really happening is that he's angry at losing our cinema sessions and the dinners we'd eat from time to time at his place before having no-strings sex. So I cut him off and declared, leave me be, you're jealous, and he said, That too, but I swear I'm calling you because I'm your friend and this kind of thing is what friends are for.

I didn't want to listen to him but I couldn't forget it and sometimes, while she was insulting me or scorning me with silence and obscene gestures, on our own or in public, I'd remember Robin, and what of course we'd never discussed again. I'd be reminded of my friend and silently ask him for help, please, please, but I was ever deeper inside, ever further from the exit. The world seemed more and more distant and I believed in myself less and less and more and more I wanted to die, more and more.

1

EVERYTHING IN NEGATIVE.

The only person in the world who dared to insult my grandmother. Without having known her. She called her a humbug. She said that my grandmother's philosophical theories were nothing more than a cowardly way of justifying her incoherent and dependent life. She dared say that.

And my mother didn't love me, she said. My mother, who had died so young and who she hadn't known either.

Not that she knows love. Ibana's never known it exists. It's as alien to her as the gods. Any god. Carnivores don't have souls. How could they have.

My sister, who'd always tried to make friends with her, was cold and a crook. My friends were all freeloaders.

That was her plant teeth gliding and closing over me.

And now you'll say, You should have got out of there.

Of course. So easy.

Exactly what I used to say before falling inside. When I was among you. Why doesn't she just leave?

But it's like climbing into a helicopter, with all that noise, and realising that only the controls manned by the other pilot work and wanting to jump but not having a parachute and not being able to see the ground because of the distance and speed. And the noise, so much noise. It's deafening. We stay put to think, we stay put to gather strength, we stay put in case something comes to mind, we don't ever believe it's forever. We stay put out of shame, because somehow you end up persuaded that you're to blame. It's not me, it's you. We stay put because we know that somehow or other it will all end. And you wait and watch and think. And think and watch and wait. At some point the carnivorous plant will be careless. Especially if we pretend we've stopped fighting, that we're no more than a shadow by now. If we mimic her gestures, her tastes, if we limit ourselves to her world and even admit that she is the maker of the little of ourselves that remains standing. If we show we are aware of being nothing, that she has saved our lives, that nothing is possible without her.

Because the promise of saving your life has always been there, in the background, since the beginning. And what does saving your life mean if not promising you there is a place where no one will ever hurt you?

No one will ever hurt you here. Come closer. And you come. No one will ever hurt you here.

Only me. But you don't say that last part.

Often that painting I made for the bow cabin of a yacht that I'd titled *No one Will Save Your Life* came to mind.

But who isn't vulnerable? Who doesn't need to let themselves fall, eyes closed and fearless, once in a while?

1

I MUST BE SHIT TO BE PUTTING UP WITH THIS SHIT. EVER MORE ashamed and more isolated.

In the beginning I used to explain, but then I started concealing it. I was afraid she'd find out. Those who had known would ask how everything was and of course I'd answer, all good, all fixed, she's like a different person, and I published saccharine lies on social media and soothed all my friends by deceiving them and stopped talking to those closest to me, those who might have found me out or guessed, those who wouldn't allow anyone to treat me that way, allow me to treat myself that way; she hated them all and she'd berate me because of them, she never stopped shouting and hitting me, insulting and abusing me and I couldn't take it any more, I was worn out, I felt like dying, all I could think about was asphyxia, loosening the slipknot a little, and the only way was to listen to her, obey her and seek refuge in the good moments she had, even though being good was no guarantee of anything, because her fits of rage could be about the present of course, but also about my past, she'd suddenly come out with one of those questions about my life, the plant's teeth tightening around the prey, and I'd give her an answer knowing in advance it was the start of another war, another one, it would be hard to breathe, I'd look around widely, everywhere and anywhere, and my response would be accompanied by a plea, please no, please no. But she was unstoppable. Her impulses of madness were like a cough in the brain, something would unleash it and then she couldn't be stopped.

And the great refrain, the trap: You provoke me. It's your fault.

But later on you observe it all carefully and see that she treats everyone who comes close enough the same way, her daughter, her mother, her sisters, her subordinates, the employees of any shop that don't satisfy her. Even her aunt told me once on the phone, you have to excuse her whims, she's like her father God rest his soul, my poor sister, what she must have suffered. I told the iguana and she almost killed me.

1

YOU KISSED ME, YOU STAY. YOU FUCKED ME, YOU TAKE ME ON. I don't fuck for the sake of it.

But that sounded good in the beginning. You see how attractive carnivorous plants are, and of course, she had a whole speech prepared that seemed like love. But it had teeth.

No one will love you like I do.

No one will understand you like I do.

No one will appreciate you like I do.

Red, green, blue, yellow, pink. All coloured pink.

She had a Messianic, passionate speech of infinite purity. She considered herself enlightened. She repeated famous lines from that bedside book and made the wisdom they exuded hers. She filled her mouth with words that had nothing to do with her life.

And when you're there, persuaded and vulnerable, the darkness comes. Her plant mouths close over you a little more. You want to think it's an exception, an accident.

You want to think that she is desperate for love.

You want to believe that something you've done has provoked her.

And that's the first big mistake.
And that's the first big mistake.
And that's the first big mistake.

SHE WAS LIKE A HAMMER.

You'd better cut your hair.

Don't wear that t-shirt.

Take shorter steps.

You're very skinny.

You're too muscular.

You exercise too much.

Stop making that gesture.

Don't talk rubbish.

Don't provoke me.

Stop talking to that friend.

Stop talking to that follower.

She on the other hand would talk to them, play nice with the friends of mine she was seeking to eradicate from my life. She'd give me well-concealed kicks if I answered, then mistreat me once we were alone.

You should give up painting and work with me. You're good at everything you do. I could help you earn more money. What you're doing now doesn't pay. It's just a pipe dream.

That was her first big mistake.

That was her first big mistake.

That was her first big mistake.

She took a risk and broke one of the filament teeth that kept the cage formed by her carnivorous mouth closed. The open gap wasn't big enough to allow me to slip out, but it let a little light in, a little fresh air. It allowed me to remember myself and the daily, invincible happiness of other times, helped me remember how I never needed to lie to anyone before, how I used to live transparently and shieldless, naked. Without noticing or even wanting it a minute portion of my old forgotten self-belief was instilled in me. I smiled at my abundant past instead of being horrified by it. For about as long as a flash of lightning.

RAGE

1

WITH GREAT EFFORT, THE OLD LADY INCHED FORWARD LITTLE by little in a broken wheelchair. She moved the half-deflated wheels with her hands and used her feet to help, the tips of which reached the ground. She was wearing slippers that had once been red and now resembled maps of the world drawn in black, brown, and yes, a faint trace of red.

She entered the corner shop to do her shopping. She wouldn't ask for much, just one of each item. She'd lived alone on the ground floor for years; the flat upstairs was abandoned and almost as damp-ridden as her home.

The owner of the shop treated her with evident care, trying not to upset her.

How is it that last week you charged me less for the same things, do you think I don't remember the prices?

She was wrong, but he preferred to go along with her, not to argue, just because.

That apple you sold me last week had a worm in it, I'll have you know.

Don't worry, madam, I'll give you another free of charge, no question, and I'm sorry.

So it was with everything. So it was every week. Luckily she was only shopping for herself.

The owner of the grocer's put it all into a bag which of course he didn't charge her for and as she'd shown him a while ago, hung it on a hook on the right side of her chair.

Take care, madam, he bid her goodbye, and thought things he couldn't say aloud but that later to unwind he'd recount to his wife, who adored hearing the horror stories her husband told her about the furious old woman.

Madam Elvira set off on her way. She headed to the hairdresser's, where she was feared more than anyone else. Suddenly, a black cat crossed the street so unexpectedly that, irritated, the old woman wanted to give it a slap. The sudden gesture knocked her shopping and as a result the bottle of oil broke. It occurred to Madam Elvira to make a claim for it from the man in the grocer's for having packed her bag so badly.

Scared, the cat was curled up in a ball not far away.

Madam Elvira moved cautiously, grabbed the stick from the space between the handles where she always kept it, and as if demons had suddenly infused her with Herculean strength she whacked the head of the feline so hard it split open. The momentum made the chair sway and it fell on its side.

Madam Elvira lay stretched out and trapped, the wheels spinning, one of her slippers flung far away, the other still on her foot. The old woman's face fell close to the smashed head of the cat. She told it, You're the same as my first husband, always in the way.

1

SHE WAS A SECT. ALL ON HER OWN SHE WAS A SECT.

How can that be, a sect of only one person? But it's not only one person. They are many, acting alone. She's one of them.

Define a sect for me. It's a secret organisation that's destructive to its followers. Voilà.

Their actions are aimed at restricting all possible freedoms, be they ideological, sexual, religious, of speech, movement, relative or associative, economic, physical, of thought or word, of affection or opinion.

They use physical or verbal violence. They seduce those within reach and sacrifice the most intimate when no one can see.

They scorn and belittle the members. They judge and terrify them. They threaten them.

Radar allows them to keep all those who could rescue the follower at a safe distance. If they get too close, they ease the pressure so the trapped person seems free. But as soon as they move away again, the punishment is doubled.

And like a sect, they take measured steps. Slow at first. Then faster. A strategy of millimetric precision. Filigree-like, a work of art. Admirable. It invites your confidence. Like when you feed a wild beast of the forest. A mouthful of food, a step forward, another mouthful, another step. The wily hidden cage, its door open. The final push is simple: one more step, the last one.

1

SHE'D HAD OTHERS, OTHER LOVERS, BETWEEN THE MALE WHO had left the iguaneenie stuck to her and me. She'd been perfecting her mechanisms. She combined them. Generally carnivorous plants use just one. In her case, she'd added more.

1. The animal is attracted by a nectar and when it rubs the plant for five seconds — you touched me, you're staying — the leaf on which it has landed closes automatically.

2. The leaves are stuck to the ground and secrete a viscous fluid resembling honey. The beast steps on it and is trapped — you fucked me, take the consequences. She curls her tentacles inwards and swallows it alive.

3. She adopts the form of a vase with a small mouth — I don't fuck for the sake of it—. The animal approaches, slips inside and when it reaches the bottom, it drowns in the watery liquid. Goodbye. In general, the beast is attracted by a nectar produced at the entrance of the trap; while walking inside, the prey seems to identify various possible ways out, but they're false, feigned solely to make it go further and further down until exhausted it falls into the liquid at the very bottom — you penetrated me, you're marrying me.

4.   When the prey moves too close to the plant, it rubs some hairs stuck to the trap. This opens and drags the animal inside — it's been years since I've been with anyone. The seal is hermetic. The swallowing begins.

5.   She also practices attraction by chemical methods with a Y-shaped leaf that allows the prey to enter but not leave — come and live at my house —. That Y-shaped house — I swear — disguised as a ship about to set sail.

When the plant has already digested the prey — or, in the unlikely event it has escaped — the trap is set again and readies herself to capture the next one.

1

YES, SOMETIMES I WANTED HER TO DIE. I SAW NO OTHER solution. Just as often as I wished death on myself.

I don't know how you reach this point. It's an exhausting labyrinth. What's it like? Dark. A low ceiling. Narrow walls. Dirty, sticky earth. It's hard to move forward. There's a continuous sound, rather high, inhuman, a jarring note on a violin. Every so often one of those blows that resonates through the body. You go around and around. Suddenly you seem to be nearing the end, everything is different and you're close to a way out. But no. Then the torture is even greater, because you've hoped, almost started breathing again.

Do you think the mosquito that comes too close to the plant is stupid? Don't you believe in chance? Are you of the opinion that some mosquitoes are more intelligent than others or do you understand that the luck of some might be different to the others?

A rush of air, heat, rain, light.

Why do you enter the labyrinth? Because you don't know what it is or because you're sure you'll come out. Why are you sure you'll come out? Because labyrinths have a way out. It's the deal. But carnivorous plants don't. You have to open one yourself. Like in a sect. As soon as you enter you lose your weapons. And you have to make them all on your own.

1

SHE CHOSE WITH CARE. SHE'D NEVER GONE TO BED WITH ANYONE who didn't bring up a few thousand results on Google.

She studied them. If they were film makers, she sought out their influences. If they were singers, she listened to their biggest hits. If they were painters, she unearthed what nourished their artistic vision. Men or women. She meticulously prepared the entrance she was making. She cunningly plotted plenty of well-chosen flattery. She practised symbiosis.

But ah, with similar or even greater skill she identified what she considered to be the prey's weaknesses. She offered help and support to mitigate them. She invested forty-eight hours a day in her mission. She took more interest in the subject than the subject did in themselves. She overwhelmed it with her delivery. Ensnared it. Savoured it. Gripped it. Bound it to her with tight, invisible thread. Adapted like a chameleon. Present, but unseen. A spider that attached to its prey to become trapped in the web she herself wove.

She hung mirrors in front, behind, above and below. Everything was the same and in that place there was only her and you.

1

YOU HAVE A MUSCLE CONTRACTURE; IT'S CALLED HONEYMOON syndrome. But the honeymoon was two years ago.

My back was painful, my neck destroyed. I had to find a way of telling her that she couldn't continue sleeping on top of me. Because that was the situation: her entire body stretched out on mine every night and her head on my left shoulder. I slept in a state of suffocation. And still, very still, so as not to wake her.

You have various contractures, the doctor, who was an old friend, told me. How do you sleep?

When I answered her, she looked at me with eyes as wide as saucers.

You're pulling my leg.

It sounded like a joke, I know.

At the beginning it seemed romantic.

You can't sleep that way. Talk to her, what's the problem?

But to explain what the problem was I'd have to explain the problem, so I told her, Done. I'll fix it. I'll talk to her today.

I stopped myself telling her that I couldn't talk to her, it would unleash a storm, telling her anything was in vain, any change would upset her.

It was a useless attempt.

Iba, I went to see Sole today. About the contracture thing. She went on the defensive. She looked at me suspiciously.

And?

She asked me how I slept.

And you said fine?

She was referring to my position.

We were sitting on the sofa, holding hands. She let go, got up and shouted:

Your friends hate me. Ever since the beginning. And the worst of it is that you don't even realise. I wonder what you told her.

The plant's acidic juices bled into everything. And the lethal injection was about to come.

I'll never sleep in your arms again. You don't love me. You haven't a clue about what I need. You don't listen to me. You're so selfish.

So that night, after subjecting me to various humiliating acts, she slept on top of me again. And my physical state continued to worsen. Slow like poison. Infallible.

1

THE PLANT WANTED THE PREY TO LOOK ONLY WITHIN.

What could there be out there to interest you? Everything you liked was a mistake, a weakness, an addiction. Everything that mattered to you before should be superfluous now you have me.

I tried to pretend, look when she couldn't see. Sometimes she caught me.

She used resources to pull me where she wanted. Presents, for example. Traps within the trap. They were balls and chains. Rucksacks disguised as parachutes. Grounded aeroplanes.

I haven't kept any of her presents. Only a watch. I've tried to exchange it for one similar, but since her gifts were very expensive — as she often let me know - I've not found a cheap version. If there's any one of you who can part with an automatic watch with a sapphire face, with numbers and a second hand, medium size, rather sporty, I'll give you this Hamilton in exchange. It's pristine.

On the subject of gifts, then. A telescope. Difficult to assemble, but even more difficult to use.

A keyboard to plug into the Mac and write.

Don't you like it? You don't like it. You never like my presents.

It was simply that she gave me things that required time. Shut in at home. Within her reach. Her presents were cages.

It's just that I don't have a lot of time.

See? You never like my presents. You always look down on what comes from me.

I didn't have a lot of time because I had to devote it to her. All of it.

1

LOOK, IBA, THIS HAVING BREAKFAST IN BED EVERY DAY AND spending two or three hours chatting about the evil in the world (and illustrating it with the friendships of mine you don't like or the anecdotes from my past you judge and casting doubt on the validity of art, given that it always depends on a ferocious ego according to you) is lovely, but I need to be more disciplined and more organised. I need to go back to the gym and get my routine back. I have to start thinking about going back to work. I need to paint.

We'd spent more than four hundred nights together and of course, more than four hundred mornings with endless breakfasts in bed.

So all this time you've been sick of it and you didn't tell me. So you've been pretending. What else are you pretending about? What else are you hiding from me?

But Iba, I've already told you, it's because of my work, it won't do itself, I have to take care of it, I have a thousand things to deliver. I can't work only when you decide to be busy. I can't live my life adapted to your schedule.

Oh, of course, the artist can't adapt to anyone, she has to do what she feels like, she, the unique and incomparable, the brilliant creator. You're pathetic. And you know what? The best thing that's come out of you is that little juvenile piece, that little painting. Everything since that is worse. You're lost in your own ego — here we go again!-, your selfishness and your pride. You don't think about anyone but yourself. And you know what? I've had it up to here. This isn't working and won't work. If you didn't want to have breakfast with me, you should have said so. Liar. You know what? It's over. I'm going — and here we were once again!

Once again I swear she packed minimal luggage and once again I swear I was begging and once again please, I was just looking for a way to express my need to get back to work, and once again please, Iba, talk to me.

I can't talk to you, Andrea. Don't you see that I can't talk to you?

And then I felt like laughing and didn't dare, because I'd already tried on other occasions to break the tension and suffered the iguana's lack of a sense of humour. The iguana was solemn, or pretentious. But never just a human being. Never. Only extremes.

So once again in the street, weighed down with bags of clothes and walking with no fixed destination, wandering as though rather than a plant rooted to a fixed place you were a dinosaur sowing destruction in its wake. If a plant, carnivorous. If a herbivore, a dinosaur. Always destruction.

Nothing more solemn than a carnivorous plant. Nothing more pretentious than a herbivore dinosaur.

1

TELL THEM WHAT YOU TOLD THOSE PEOPLE THE OTHER DAY.

Me obeying. And her:

She's so intelligent, so brilliant, so special, unique, she's incredible, the things she comes up with, the flights of fancy she has, I've never known anyone like her, it's impossible to be bored with her, blah blah blah.

Me blushing. People looking away. Her persisting, making the love she professes clear, how much admiration she feels, how grateful she is to fate for having found me and me choosing her blah blah blah.

Tell them that thing with the bank. Tell them that thing on the trip. Tell them that thing with the present. Tell them. Tell them.

Not daring to contradict her. And telling, telling. And thinking, why don't you tell them? Why do I have to say what you tell me to?

And she goes on and on saying marvellous things about me to people in the third person, as if I'm not there.

I'm thinking, if they knew, if I could tell them what I really should tell, how she treats me at home, how trapped I feel, how

I've lost my will and sleep and appetite, how she belittles me, how I live in fear of upsetting her, because upsetting her means shouts and shoves and insults and slamming doors and a lot of noise and a lot of fear. And I know intuitively the more I take the more of a prisoner I am. No, I can't allow that, I have to find the way out. There has to be one.

As Tom Walker sings, there must be angels.

Then when one of those encounters ended, Do you think I didn't notice how you tried to be the centre of attention? Without fail. What do you want people to think? You make me look bad. There I am saying how much I love you and you intent on telling your ridiculous artist anecdotes. You're pathetic.

1

THE PROBLEM IS THAT YOU'RE TIRED AND YOU DON'T KNOW IT. You're not capable of seeing how you feel. And it's natural. Because you've lived life depending on what others say and doing what they want. That's how they've abused and still abuse your generosity and trust. And that's why you have such parasitical friends and family. You should observe this fatigue of yours you can't see.

But what fatigue are you talking about, Iba? I feel very well, don't worry, really, I feel very well.

It was obvious my energies were at full strength. If there's one thing that has distinguished and distinguishes me it's unfailing enthusiasm, which the iguana only managed to banish at the end of our so-called relationship which should rightly be christened a kidnapping.

See? You never listen to what I say.

But I'm not tired, Iba, really I'm not.

You're tired. Very tired. You have to tell me how you are.

Do you understand why I sometimes still felt like laughing even though I didn't dare?

Do you understand why I sometimes still had the damn hope she might realise she was a carnivore and not a humble lily with a wide mouth and pistils and suspiciously shaped teeth?

ABUSE

THERE ARE TWO WAYS OF UNDERSTANDING THIS, HE TELLS HER. One is mine and the other is yours. So to save ourselves the bother, let's agree that there's only one way of understanding it.

She doesn't speak. She's sitting on the bed, dressed in a t-shirt, socks and flat, sporty shoes. She shakes her head. She can't be here. This isn't happening.

We already talked about it, he states.

That's not true, she thinks.

I paid for your ticket here and it was obvious you had to pay me back.

He came to meet her at the airport. He kissed her. They kissed as soon as they saw one another. I couldn't wait for you to get here, he said to her. Then they went straight to that dark apartment full of dark rooms, with fake windows drawn on the dirty walls.

Is this your home? she wanted to ask, but she waited, she said, I think it'd be better if we go to a hotel for the first few days, I'll feel more comfortable, I have a little bit of money saved up. She was terrified. That six foot man with whom she had chatted for a year didn't seem like the delicate, cultured architect who hadn't only shown interest in her, but also in her painting, her artistic career. I think you'd have opportunities here. I have good friends in the world of galleries, contacts.

A year of dreaming and finally he persuaded her to come. I'll pay for your ticket, and if that makes you feel bad, don't fret, I love you, you can pay me back.

It was another line. How could I have been such an idiot.

The man left all her belongings in a room at the back, before responding, A hotel, how did that occur to you. Then he grabbed her by the hand and brought her to the room where they are now. He said, Now I'll try you out, and he took off her skirt and socks and raped her. Then he got up and said, Very good, now time to work. Here. And he held out a pill and a glass with a transparent liquid that, as she instantly confirmed when there was no alternative to swallowing it because he threatened to beat her if she didn't, wasn't water but vodka.

This can't be happening, she thinks, she's not able to cry and even less able to shout as he tells her, I already have the first client waiting.

The rules are clear. Don't answer any personal questions. Don't say your real name, or think of asking for help. I'll be watching you.

She tries to think quickly. She's dazed by the vodka and the pill. The client comes in. The architect leaves the room after shaking his hand and receiving a fine wad of notes.

Lie down, the newcomer tells her as he lowers the zip of his trousers. Open up, he orders her.

While she has him inside her, she whispers her real name in his ear, her real surnames, her real situation, asks him for help in a barely audible voice, almost faint, please, whoever you are, help me, she says, because she doesn't know, she can't know the man has paid to strangle her as he fucks her.

The last painting she'd painted was titled *The First Kiss I Give You* and arrived hours later, wrapped with extreme care, at the false address the architect had given her.

1

HER OPINIONS WEREN'T OPINIONS. THEY WERE COMMANDS.

Don't you think it would be better for you not to go to the conference?

She meant don't go. She meant, if you go I don't matter to you; you're an idiot; you have an oversized ego; you want to be out of sight; you're looking for a lover; you're already unfaithful to me; who will you see at this conference; right now I'm so looking forward to us going to the cinema to see the film I told you about (that she hadn't told me about); are you going?

Who would dare?

Never mind. It's not so important. Never mind. This way she'll calm down. Never mind. This way she won't shout. Never mind. This way we'll be at peace.

Like a virus, unstoppable.

Do you know that viruses are the only living things that risk devastating the place they inhabit despite this leading to their own destruction? They attack without mercy. When the conquered body is about to be definitively wiped out, the virus tries to emigrate to another to repeat the process. Viruses are nourished by destruction.

1

SHE SAYS, I DON'T LIKE MY WORK. I FEEL DIVIDED. IT DOESN'T square with my principles.

I say, you're right, not really; that is, it doesn't square with the principles you say you have. Having principles helps us do what we believe, not just say it. If for example you declare you don't trust the capitalist system and yet you work in banking — just an example — you're lying to yourself. It seems to me you do believe in the capitalist system but you don't like the image it reflects of you. I don't know, I say, to finish.

Do you realise you take any chance in conversation to put me down?

Thinking, why didn't I bite my tongue, why did I once again believe she wanted to have a conversation, why don't I leave her and put an end to this torture, why did I marry this woman, why?

The mistake is asking why. We'll never know. It's like approaching a bird of prey wanting to find out why it flies. Watching her hoping to understand. It won't happen. She'd sooner scratch out our eyes while we watch her. In a dazed moment of carelessness.

1

I DON'T THINK I LOVE THE IGUANEENIE, SHE BLURTS OUT ONE day. And I don't think the iguaneenie loves me either.

What do you mean you don't love each other? I say, What do you mean you don't love each other if you're mother and daughter? The thing is you've lived just the two of you all this time, perhaps the lines of your relationship have become blurred.

The poor iguaneenie is nothing more than an appendage to the changeable and irascible orders of the iguana. She'd shut herself up in her dirty, messy room, and sleep all the hours she could, waiting for her mother to go on a business trip again before poking her head out into the land of the living. From time to time a boyfriend would visit, as dirty and messy as her. The iguana had chosen him to keep her daughter entertained. They only emerged to go to the toilet, not even closing the door. Or to the fridge.

How have the lines become blurred? You don't have a clue, and she repeated 'a clue' in large capitals, of what it's like to raise a daughter all alone, the effort it takes, how it hinders you and shapes your life, how it nullifies you, how it makes you disappear from everything and everyone. You don't have a clue, and she repeated 'a clue' in large capitals, of the inhuman sacrifice required. How dare you belittle maternity that way. How dare you question the way we live and have lived. Don't even think, and she repeated 'Don't even think' in large capitals, of messing with my daughter. Don't you dare!

I was silent of course thinking, Poor daughter, she has to get away or she'll swallow her up. She's used her as a support for everything, told her all her problems, abandoned her every time she's had a sexual passion and ingested her again once she's gobbled down the latest trapped beast. Carnivores can only take on one prey at a time.

So she had her cornered. She left her with her grandmother, her father, her sisters, whoever, until the daughter could stay alone with computers, addicted to computers like a carnivore, calling them mama. And I was thinking, Run, iguaneenie, take advantage of her having me between her teeth. Run, go, because once she's swallowed me, she'll feast again on you.

But of course, if you were born inside a carnivorous plant tell me what you would do. What you would do.

Finally, she took advantage of my coming, and I helped her. The iguana opened her throat to trap me and before it closed completely I shouted to her, Now, run, leave, get out of here. Frightened, the poor iguaneenie escaped, all the while hating me for having taken her place. Just like the male specimen with whom she'd been conceived had escaped one day, just after she was born and the plant was occupied with her new toy: the baby carnivore.

1

I ENTERED THE HOUSE. THERE WAS A SILENCE LIKE CHILLED mash. Solid. Her bag on the hanger by the entrance, beside her jacket.

I called, Iba?

There was no answer. A piece of chicken on the counter in the kitchen. Beside it a knife, an open tin of tomatoes, a sliced carrot.

Iba?

The blind of our bedroom up, the windows wide open, the bed unmade. A wooden spoon on the bedside table.

No longer shouting but in a whisper, Iba?

I began to sweat. And my throat dried up.

I reached the living room. The shutters were open. One of the doors was banging against the wall because of the wind. I went out onto the balcony. But beforehand I looked behind me. Then I saw her. She disappeared. She saw me see her disappear. Iba?

I retraced my steps. I went towards the sound. She was in the kitchen. The chicken in a pan, with the tomatoes and carrot, and her in an apron, stirring with the wooden spoon that had been on the bedside table. I said nothing to her. I went to the bedroom. The bed was already made, the window closed, the blind half-lowered.

I returned to the balcony. I closed the shutters and looked directly into the sun. I couldn't be more blind.

1

WE BOUGHT A SOUND SYSTEM FOR THE BAKERY SHE WANTED TO open after she was kicked out of the world of finance in which she'd moved like a rotten egg in a glass of water: floating. She wanted to focus on making bread in different shapes.

The shop was called Bread & Circus.

I helped her make the project a reality. I provided her with all the contacts and a good chunk of money earned by what she called my unprofitable calling.

People were charmed by the shapes she made. They didn't know that they were empty inside.

'I'll feed all your bodies with bread that nourishes your souls.'

She started saying things like that. She copied them from a book, the same one she'd used in the business world the first two years we were together. Four years in all. She'd learn them by heart and recite them as if they were her ideas. People were fascinated; they ate her bread of air and were filled with nothing. They looked like balloons, all of them. They made you want to puncture them with a needle.

The sound system in question wasn't expensive; it looked good. It made a faint hissing sound. Hardly noticeable. But the perfect mechanisms of a carnivore detect the slightest malfunction and feel annoyed.

We'll return it, she said.

We can't expect any more for the price we paid, I said.

Your problem is always accepting things as they are, she accused me.

Let's go, then.

The people in the shop knew me. Or mostly me. In that town where she remained afterwards to defame me from behind the counter of the bakery they mostly knew me.

They were happy to see me. Although not so much when she began complaining.

You have no right to sell defective products. This is fraud.

Me smiling as if nothing was wrong.

The boy in the shop smiling as if nothing was wrong.

Her, I want you to give me my money back.

We can't, the boy informed her. We can exchange the system for another of the same model. We'd have it in a week.

Firstly, I don't plan on waiting a week. Secondly, what's that plural you used all about, we can't, who can't? What's wrong with you? Do you identify with this piddly 'business'?

She said piddly business in that belittling way. And went on.

I find this treatment intolerable, and she repeated 'intolerable' in large capitals. Obviously I regret making the mistake of purchasing here.

She looked at me.

The boy was mortified. Like me, he wanted the ground to swallow him up from pure adjacent embarrassment. He said, I'm not allowed to refund a product that works.

That works? Works! she shouted, and looked around at everyone in that big place which luckily wasn't too many at that time in the morning.

I'm leaving, she stated.

I shrugged my shoulders, picked up the system, followed her, silently apologised to the boy.

While going out she attacked me. Apologising to him! I saw you, do you think I didn't see you? What the fuck is wrong with you?

He's working, Iba, it's his job, the boy doesn't ...

Go in there and tell him, go on, tell him you're incapable, and she repeated 'incapable' in large capitals, of standing up for us, standing up for our rights, that you're a wimp, with no self-esteem, a good for nothing, and to top it all you think yourself empathetic and tolerant, and it's all ego, that enormous ego of yours.

We were back there again.

Of course I felt like letting the heavy apparatus fall to the ground, getting rid of it just like all that shit she was hurling into me as if I were a dumpster but, surprising as it may seem, as it seems even to me, I pulled the car keys out of my jeans pocket as best I could, pressed them to open the boot, put my burden in, and asked, Want to drive?

She didn't even answer. She always drives, I thought, even if she's not at the wheel.

1

PEOPLE LOOK AT YOU IN DISBELIEF. ALL THEIR ENQUIRIES SEEM directed to understanding how a woman like you fell into such a snare as this. They're not aware of the accusation buried in that question. It's like asking a bear why it stepped on the metal trap hidden among leaves that's now clenched around one of its paws. What should it have done? Remain in its cave forever more? Wait for others to bring it food, fresh air, news from the world? If you're alive, you're in danger.

To you it looks like you're emerging from the cave. And it so happens that you fall into a well. A never-ending well. Further and further from the light. You fall down to where there is no way out. You can't breathe. You're gasping like a fish out of water. You're out of your element. The hook destroying your mouth. The shot in the middle of the forehead. The trap criss-crossing your flesh. The rope tying your paws. The net around you. An animal with no natural movement, a puppet, a trophy.

Dying. Stunned.

1

SHE'D SAY, LOOK AT THE BREAD, SEE ITS ABILITY TO MAKE SHAPES, change its image, adapt.

She identified with the bread. What she meant was in fact, Look at me, look at my ability to make shapes, change my image, adapt.

She'd invite people to the bakery and show them the dexterity with which she kneaded the dough, her hands covered in flour and sweat dripping down her forehead.

She'd say, It's you that puts limits on life and not life putting limits on you. Try to push beyond them.

She'd say, There are three things that can't be hidden forever: the sun, the moon and the truth, and I knew they were phrases she'd underlined that morning in the only book she ever studied.

She'd say it all with a home-spun, religious peace that made it impossible to imagine the blood she was hiding.

Every time she delivered a sculpture of bread, she'd say, may my spirit be with you.

At home at night, as she was counting takings, she'd say, I'd never have thought the spirit business would bring in so much cash. And she'd laugh.

1

PLANTS ARE MORE FLEXIBLE THAN HUMANS, NO MATTER HOW carnivorous they are.

You only needed to see her bend and contort herself in bed. A ballerina. I'd ask her to leave her heels on, blindfold her, tie her up. She liked us to pretend that she was the one trapped by me.

She'd open up her stigma to me, wrap me in her corollas, seduce me with her filaments, attract me with her anthers, caress me with her petals, screw me with her stem until finally, she'd offer me her full, sweet calyx.

She seemed to be other things. A wise tree, the sap of the wise tree, the cloud that gives it shade, the rain that quenches its thirst, the mountain where it can be found, the cry of the earth in which it sinks, the roots that sustain it, the hurricane that can't pull it out, the lightning that doesn't split it, the bark scrawled with so-and-so loves so-and-so in a heart, the ants that cross it and the birds that sleep on it, the light that penetrates its leaves and the sound they give to the breeze, the seed that gives it life and the embrace of the one who approaches it. She seemed the truth and depth of the tree. Everything but a carnivorous plant, understand?

1

DINNER. SHE HAS A FATAL TRAP READY. A QUESTION, A COMMENT, a threat to choke me. It's always like this, but I forget every time. She places branches to cover the well and shouts to me from the other side. I fall for it.

If you could do anything now, what would you like to do?

I enjoy hypotheses, what-if conversations, fiction. I step confidently onto the false ground of the covered hole.

I'd love to go to meditate in India for a month.

Go then, she retorts. I begin to fall. In vain I scrabble at the freshly made mud walls which disintegrate in my fists.

You asked what I would do. I don't know, that's how I understood it.

You don't understand anything. You only think about yourself. How can you even consider travelling to India or wherever without me?

At the bottom of the well, looking up, in pain from the impact, shaking my head no, covering myself with my arms to protect myself from what would soon fall on top of me.

You don't understand anything because you're selfish; an egocentric egotist. She said it as she put her mobile in her pocket, her arms into her sleeves and threaded her way through the dark wooden tables in her white overcoat, a wolf in lamb's clothing.

VIOLENCE

THE TEENAGERS WAITED IN THE CHANGING ROOMS. THEY'D ALL had the same dream since touching a ball for the first time. They knew that among the crowd watching the match that day there would be some managers and scouts from the greatest teams in the world.

Of course, both teams had a captain. The one from the blue team was Damian. The one from the red team was Ben. Their names are imaginary, because this involves minors. Boys who at that time were minors.

Until the thirty-second minute of the first half everything had transpired with the bottled-up tension of inevitable rivalry, but in the thirty-third minute a beautiful play by Damian, supported by a choreography of centre-backs and mid-fielders that seemed rehearsed to perfection, allowed the blues to reach the box, confound the enemy and score a triumphant goal, one of those goals that humiliates the opponent with its accuracy. Not only that: they've not touched the ball for the whole game, and to cap it all the ball reached the keeper by going through the ridiculous truncated x shape formed by his lowered knees as he tried to avert disaster.

The roar from the stands was deafening, especially to Ben who refused to cover his ears so as not to betray his irritation. It was with great difficulty that he didn't hurl himself on Damian to punch him when they were in mid-field to restart the game.

The rest of the first half passed off with no change to the score. The referee noted a few fouls and everyone went to the changing rooms.

The second half wasn't very different. At first. Ball possession was fifty-fifty. The blues were playing a little more conservatively, reassured by the one-nil score. The reds committed unforced errors for the same reason. In the eighty-seventh minute, when the match seemed more or less over and some spectators had even stood up to leave, one of the reds, who had cleverly stolen the ball from the blues during one of their few offensives, shook off his nerves. Then that unmistakable murmur of the build-up to a goal could be heard.

The midfielders impeccably covering Ben. The unbeatable position of the forward near the box. The perfect angle to take the fatal shot. The keeper was shouting, giving useless, desperate orders.

Slow motion.

Ben prepares to kick the ball. He gauges the arc correctly. At the same time, the midfielder marking Damian stumbles into him and they both fall. The referee doesn't stop play, he doesn't see any foul. Damian's head falls just beside the ball, Ben doesn't think twice. A kick with unusual force, with a power that, had it been the ball, it would have been the goal everyone in the stands was waiting for.

1

OF COURSE THE DAY CAME WHEN I NO LONGER FELT LIKE answering the phone and didn't even dare to. It might be someone who could unleash a war. Another one. My main state was one of exhaustion. Besides, I didn't want to answer in plural. I was ashamed to say we're fine when someone who barely knew her would call to find out how I was. They'd say hello, how are you doing, and I'd say we're fine, getting by, we're going on holiday, our feet sting, we feel like pissing.

So we don't want to see your sister or this friend of yours or that acquaintance. So we won't answer that, we won't decide this or accept those. So you're an appendage, I have you, forget about you.

A full list of forbidden things.

An empty list of those permitted.

Don't talk to strangers, don't cross the street, don't read, don't go sailing, stop painting, make bread on my orders, remember you've done it all badly, no one loves you, they've only got close to you because of a kind of misplaced idolatry of an art for which by the way you have no talent, you're nothing, stay where I tell you to, don't make me angry, don't make me immobilise you with more traps, don't make me be like this, don't provoke me, it's obvious you're an impostor, stay still in the damned well once and for all, I'm sick and tired of it, your sick desire to go back to that repulsive past that pursues you, you promiscuous sinner.

It took me so long to understand she was talking about herself. She'd slept around for money, for work, out of fear. It took me so long to understand that it was she who was the fraud. It took me so long to understand that the well in which she'd thrown me was her own unhappiness.

1

WHY DIDN'T YOU SAY ANYTHING TO ME? MY SISTER WOULD ACCUSE me one day.

Why didn't you tell me? my friend X would accuse me one day.

Why didn't you tell me? my friend H would accuse me one day.

Those were my dreams. Leaving and being accused of not reporting her.

Why don't we report them?

It's very difficult to understand that while the torture comes from without the only place to cut it off is within. It must be stopped by the capacity to endure. To hope. To believe.

The monster is within. It's the one justifying the abuse.

1

SHE NEVER LEFT ME ALONE. NOT FOR A MOMENT.

Where are you going?

Answer: the toilet.

Thoughts in the toilet: Gofuckyourselfyourottenbitch, I'm going to the toilet, for fuck sake I'm going three steps, to the door over there, want to stick your hands in there and check I'm pissing?

What are you thinking?

Answer: nothing.

Thoughts: What the fuck do you care what I'm thinking, if I say you'll insult me, offend me, ridicule me, criticise me, you'll talk about you you you, and tell me that I'm not present with you and you're always thinking about me and you truly love me, so much you've expelled mother, daughter, sisters and holy spirit from your life.

Against my opinion and wishes, for fuck sake, my wish was for you to continue having mother, daughter, sisters and holy spirit, fucking hell, so you'd have them for you and not impose them on me, that you might enjoy them and let me enjoy my repulsive emotional world that doesn't even touch the soles of your shoes you immaculate Roman Catholic apostolic girl against abortion married in the Church in the first flush of youth and pregnant shortly after by a husband whose last name you of course adopted until he fled in terror as you stared at the scrap of meat he'd made for you that had just come out of you and you were unable to love.

But no. To control my world she had to abandon hers. You see? I sacrifice everything for you. I don't need anything else.

It must be remembered carnivorous plants swallow only one prey at a time.

1

SOMETIMES IN THE FIRST TWO YEARS, BEFORE THE BAKERY, SHE would go on trips for work. Her daughter and I used to breathe sighs of relief. Each of us doing our own thing. No more shouting, suspicions, instructions, orders. She'd play her computer games, I'd paint with whatever colours I felt like, without the iguana telling me I was making bad choices. We'd eat together and have deep conversations, we'd smoke inside the house — marijuana for her and tobacco for me — and we didn't have to lie. There were days I played with her, she taught me tricks, and days she asked me to look at her drawings, to see what I thought. They were good. The iguaneenie would be splendid once she managed to escape from the plant. That's what I thought. And I was right.

These were times of ceasefire.

The iguana controlled us by surprise calls on the phone. She left us with orders to watch one another. She'd ask her what I was doing and with whom. She'd ask me what she was doing and how. Her mission was to set us against each other. She couldn't permit our alliance. She had to make us believe we were rivals. There's not enough space for two prey in the heart of a carnivorous plant.

When Ibana went away there was air in the house, whether we had the windows open or not. A fresh wind from the sea, from the desert, from the mountain. It was always daytime, whether it was night or day.

Sooner or later the peace would end, on her return. Recklessly, the iguaneenie would ask, When are you going away next? I thought it too, but I used to say, we missed you so much, hopefully you'll never have to go away again. By that stage I already knew that lying kept me close to the way out.

And back to war.

1

SOMETIMES YOU THINK EVERYTHING MIGHT CHANGE BECAUSE she tells you she wasn't aware of what she was doing, and assures you she's understood and asks for forgiveness kissing your every wound in a kind of paroxysm of repentance, and begs for another chance and promises that you're right, swears never again, pleads fear and insecurity, traumatic experiences; a childish mother and a violent father and a lying daughter from an unfaithful man. These moments are few, and they're not genuine. They're intentional. Means to an end. They all form part of the trap. They're like the words of a compulsive gambler, who promises they won't go back when they lose, but as soon as they recover they forget what they've said. They swear only until they have enough money to place another bet.

What type of stake should be plunged into a heart that doesn't welcome feelings but intentions?

1

BETTER YOU DON'T COME. IT'LL BE A BIG FUSS, AND I'LL BE BUSY, so busy, so many people coming over to say hi. That's what I told her. It was the opening of my exhibition. The most important of my life up to then.

I was reminded of all the artists, philosophers, doctors persecuted by the Church. She is the Church. She is the sect. A one-person sect.

She came, of course. She had to keep an eye on me.

I can close the bakery. Nobody'll die of hunger for a couple of days.

She despised her followers. They weren't the class of people she wanted. They ate hungrily with no manners or elegance, she'd say. They don't praise the sculptures I create enough, she declared. Old, fat, who cares. Like me, she really took them in. She believed she did sacred work, as if the bread sculptures were Eucharistic hosts.

She came and tried to sour what should have been one of the happiest days of my whole existence for me.

While she was en route, she called my mobile nonstop while I couldn't answer. And when I did have two minutes to go to the toilet and, stressed, returned her call, she used the time to ask me: why don't you answer, who are you with. She used it to complain that she couldn't find anywhere to park and I didn't care.

She bit my face that time. She left a circular, red mark where my blood had risen to defend me against her teeth. The following day I had an interview. I covered up the barbarity — for which she didn't apologise in the least — with make-up as best I could. While posing for photos, I turned the other cheek.

Why had she bitten me?

Because after the opening we'd gone out for dinner with some friends. Among them was my ex, the tall one, who told an anecdote about a day I'd made a fool of myself, as a kind of counter-balance.

The iguana's conclusion? That story was told deliberately, to exclude her, keep her on the margins. My mistake according to her? Not having marked my territory with an opportune interruption or contemptuous expression.

Once on the street after leaving the restaurant, the plant opened her mouth, and pretending she wanted to give me a kiss, she sank her teeth into my skin. The pain was so intense I can still feel it. I close my eyes and feel sick. I open them and feel horrified.

1

I KNOW ENOUGH SECRETS ABOUT HER TO BLOW HER REPUTATION to shreds. I've never told them. I never will. What I do know is that there are things that just can't be done. I'll not use a needle to puncture the bread.

1

SHE SOLD HER CAR BECAUSE MINE USED LESS PETROL AND SPENT the whole time my imprisonment lasted complaining about having decided to share the money she'd got with me and the iguaneenie. (Later she made us pay tenfold.)

I spent all the money my friends gave me for our wedding on our honey(bile)moon, and it's about time I say something on the matter.

Because your friends didn't give us anything. Remember, Iba? They attended the meal with gusto, that's all.

1

HELLO IBA, I KNOW YOU WON'T READ THIS POLICE STATEMENT about the damages you caused me. Statement, not report. It's too late to report.

Name and Surname
Nickname
Place of birth
Date of birth
Identity document
Sex/gender
Occupation
Hospital admissions
Insurance Coverage
Telephone

Fill it in yourself, Iba. Take a good look at it.

- Account of the Facts
- Makeup of the Cohabiting Family Group
- Kinds of violence

a) Physical
b) Psychological
- Frequency of acts of violence
- Was the victim pregnant?
- Was the victim disabled?

Perpetrator
- Criminal record?
- Alcoholism?
- Substance abuse?
- Psychiatric treatment?
- Mental illness?
- Weapons?
- Weapons for the purposes of intimidation?
- Threats?
- Compulsive gambler?
- History of familial violence?

I'll answer just one thing, Iba:

Did she compel you to write a will leaving everything in her name?

Yes.

ISOLATION

THE FATHER AND MOTHER ARE FED UP WITH THE SEVEN-YEAR-OLD boy they call son, because although it's hard to believe and they'd never wanted one they have him. Have as in the verb 'to have' but not as in the verb I like sharing my life with a growing being that depends on me and needs me and I must educate.

Because he's part of their property, they decide the way to keep him entertained so he's least annoying is to give him a computer that even NASA doesn't have, a more powerful internet connection than the CIA, and a screen any IMAX cinema would envy.

But one week, one of the many we use to escape, they decide to take him away with them. A red-letter day, the kind that will prove to us we're up to snuff, we're happy, everything is going tickety-boo and we're not on the verge of killing each other or even ourselves. It takes them three seconds to realise their error. The child has no computer here, or internet, any insulation at all.

They ask at the hotel reception. We assume there must be something for children? No, we don't have anything. But faced with the united vehement fury emanating from the couple's gaze, the person at reception has an idea and blurts it out without thinking. This time of year there are lots of silkworms in the mulberry woods we have out the back. They're harmless, we can look for a shoebox for him and he can play there, boys like looking at them, taking care of them, thinking about feeding them, and with the stay you have left he'll have time to see them make cocoons, so I believe, he'll surely like it and not bother you. She realises she shouldn't have said this, voicing aloud what they themselves keep secret, so she immediately remedies it with, It'll be educational, it's great that you asked, parents in general don't bother seeking proper entertainment for their kids and cart them around all day, poor little ones, what torture. Reconciled to themselves, the couple smile. What a talent for hearing what they want and nothing else, thinks the girl, but of course she says nothing, simply goes looking for a shoebox. Luckily she has one from a pair she bought a few days before, when her heel had broken while she was working and she'd left the box there, she hadn't thrown it away. Just in case. Sometimes what you do for no reason ends up being the most useful, she thinks.

Mother, father and receptionist accompany the child, who walks with short steps, to the garden of mulberry trees. Head down, dragging his feet, his unwilling hands in his parents' on both sides. He'd prefer to put his hands in his pockets and he'd like to whistle, but he knows both things annoy them. They are the first things he does when he's left all alone with the box full of worms the receptionist herself has plucked from the trees.

And then, as he whistles, not knowing the reason or even asking himself why, he grabs each of the worms in his little nail-bitten fingers and decapitates them before throwing them far away, the heads in one direction and the bodies in another.

He leaves only one in the box. Just one. He stares at it as if he's trying to understand a chemical formula or the formation of the wind. The worm doesn't even move, perhaps scared by the disappearance of the others. Or because it has no reason to do so.

No one asks him about the worms. Every day after breakfast they leave him in the mulberry wood with a sandwich and drink for lunchtime, and they come to find him in the evening, at dinnertime. Afterwards he goes to bed alone in his room.

After breakfast on the last day they tell him, Say goodbye to your worms, little Marcel, we're leaving today.

Little Marcel and his box in the wood. Little Marcel opens the lid. He whistles. He grabs the worm, takes off its head, flings it far away and leaves the rest of the body in the box where for the first time he sees it moving in search of something.

They come to find him. Little Marcel continues to whistle. When his parents offer him their hands little Marcel puts his in the back pockets of his trousers.

1

LET'S SPEAK FOR A MOMENT OF THE WITNESSES TO THE FACTS, the people who knew, who saw it. Some of them faithful clients of the bakery by now.

A string of cowards. Business people. Merchants.

I have no words for you. You saw what you saw and yet there you stayed. Accomplices to torture.

Why?

Deep down you believe: She must have done something.

You all identify with the plant.

Honourable judges, you are the rapists.

Why believe in horror if it's not exercised against your own persons, right?

She didn't hit me.

She didn't insult me.

She didn't abuse me.

She didn't rape me.

She didn't because not me.

Not. Me.

She. She must have done something. Her.

Nothing to add. Enjoy your gowns, your lordships.

My nudity hides nothing.
Look up the word loyalty in the dictionary.

1

HARDLY ANY GARDENERS OR FLORISTS LOVE CARNIVORES. NO one eagerly anticipates their arrival. They are identified to be isolated.

Sometimes someone confuses a species. Often when they realise it's too late.

1

YOU LEARN TO VOMIT INWARDS. AND TO FEEL DIZZINESS inwards too. You pray, if you know how. And if not, you make up the words. You talk to yourself. Inwards, always. You say things like, now this is unbearable, like what a pain. You advise yourself, stay quiet, stay quiet, stay quiet. This is very normal, you know? Because you reach a point where you don't talk to anyone.

Do I believe that it benefitted my work somehow? That old chestnut about suffering stimulating creation. Everything I couldn't express is there. The fear. The reflections, the images. The colours, the desperation. Painting was the only place of calm. It was hard for me to defend, but it was very clear to me that it was the last line to be crossed. She did try, the plant. She tried to destroy it all. I took the flak. Black, immense, overwhelming.

There came a point when I saw her as an elephant hunter, a lion hunter. She comes out with a weapon to make a kill. She can't bear freedom she doesn't have. It offends her. She rides dogmas, not principles. She repeats them. And she needs others to obey her to make them true.

Empathy? Of course I feel it. No sympathy, though.

1

IN THIS GAME OF LIFE, THE BRAVE PERSON DARES TO DO WHAT is necessary.

That's what I thought, and I told myself, You have to get out of here however you can. Think. And I began to study. The first thing was to understand that an object susceptible to being devoured by a carnivorous plant cannot love the plant up close and must acknowledge some kind of disorder if she falls in love with it.

The frog's mistake: trusting the scorpion and putting it on its back to cross the river. The scorpion's mistake: trusting what he wants rather than what he is and drowning after stabbing the frog with its poisonous stinger while they are in the water. Hope is a trap.

1

CONTROL IS LIKE A STONE IN YOUR SHOE.

The holy inquisition. The holy interrogation. What would you do? How would you answer? With the truth? You already know when the inquisitors don't receive the answer they require they move straight to torture, don't you? And you already know if torture doesn't produce the desired effect — a sincere change of mind — the stake follows, don't you?

Why did you go out with that woman?

Why are you wearing those jeans?

Who took this photo of you?

Where are you going?

What are you thinking?

What did you do to them in bed?

What do they think of me?

Why do you say 'I' and not 'we'?

What would you like to do if you could?

What are you thinking right now?

Why did you like the French woman so much?

Give me the password for your mobile. Your laptop. The PINs of your credit cards.

Don't you trust me?

Why do your students write you emails?

Are you trying to get her into bed?

Why are you so nice to people you don't know?

What are you thinking?

Didn't such a superficial person disgust you?

Who was that message from?

What do they want from you?

How can you be so gullible?

Are you an idiot or just act like one?

Do you really think you're a good painter?

Why don't you face up to them and say no?

How could you have ignored me in this?

What are you thinking about?

Where are you?

Why are you late?

Who are you with?

Where are you coming from?

What are you thinking?

Are you telling me the truth?

Are you sure you didn't go to bed with that one?

Are you sure she's not hitting on you?

Why have you had so many lovers?

How can I know that you love me?

Is doing this and that to show me that you really love me?

What are you thinking about?

Who's called you today?

Can't you see she wants to fuck you?

Who have you been talking to, to say that to me now?

Are you really going to finish this painting like that?

Who's directing you?

Do you think I believe you?

What are you thinking?

Don't you want to be with me any more?

Don't you see you're making a fool of yourself?

Don't you think you've painted enough?

Do you think you're really funny?

How can you be so illogical?

How can you think that?

How can you say that?

How can you not agree with me?

Don't you see that it's you that provokes me?

Don't you see you drive me up the wall?

Don't you realise you never stop lying to yourself?

Who called you just now?

Why don't you answer your phone?

Do you have to answer your phone now?

Do you have to sort that now?

Do you have to tidy that now?

Don't you see they don't love you?

What are you thinking?

1

I THOUGHT ABOUT THE BOA ROBIN HAD TOLD ME ABOUT.

A woman had one. It had been off its food for a number of days.

She brought it to the vet, who with no preamble asked her, Does it sleep with you?

She said yes.

Has it been wrapping itself around you over the last few days, by any chance?

Yes, admitted the woman. Strange, because it's never done that before, she added. It completely envelops me, completely. Poor thing. It's seeking comfort.

The vet informed her: It's taking your measurements to eat you.

1

EVERYTHING IS FRAGMENTARY. THERE'S NO ORDER. PREY LOSE any notion of time. Everything is the same. But when we reached year three I knew I found myself in the last moments before being devoured.

That is terror. And terror paralyses you.

I couldn't call her ex-husband to find out how he'd escaped. He was a good guy. I'd met him many years before when he'd interviewed me about one of my exhibitions. I got on well with him. A journalist, serious. But he might give me false information in order to keep me prisoner and save his daughter, who'd gone to live with him. There was no space for two prey in the plant's trap.

Nor did I dare contact any of her ex-lovers, who according to the iguana were a string of mentally ill persons who had mistreated and undervalued her. They had taken advantage of her and her money.

The money thing is interesting. She claimed that it didn't interest her in the slightest but she'd always sweep home and sacrifice the principles she defended in words by her acts, to have as much of it as possible. She sold the air inside the bread thanks to the shapes she wrapped around it.

It occurred to me that perhaps this was what she'd learned from her parents. Nouveau riche, also merchants. Not living up to what you identify with is very complicated. You scramble to accumulate it when you think it's about quantity.

1

NOT KNOWING WHERE TO MOVE SO AS NOT TO MAKE IT WORSE, not die, still have an opportunity to escape; damaged but alive; mutilated but able; wounded but taking a stand.

Staying scared me. I'd lost the will. I'd not be capable of escaping if I waited much longer. But escaping scared me. And asking for help scared me. And trying and failing scared me. I feared reprisals. I found it hard to breathe. I'd started forgetting life. She used to give me some of that bread of hers to anaesthetise me. And when I didn't eat it, she accused me, she threatened me. There was bread everywhere at home. She'd put the brushes and canvases away. The paintings. It's not like you're painting right now. It's not like you'll be painting anyway, we have work in the bakery. You said you'd help me, didn't you?

1

A FRIEND TOLD ME ONCE THAT SUGAR CAN STOP HAEM-
orrhages.

What stops the actions that cause wounds?

IMMOLATION

A WOMAN LIVING ALONE IN A HOUSE IN THE COUNTRY, ISOLATED from everything and everyone, received a tiger as a present. A cub. She could hold it if she made a cradle of her two hands. And kiss it, embrace it, play with it and sleep with it.

The woman was happy with her new companion. She loved his stripes, his endless eyes, his sighs and snores.

The first roar scared her. She got used to it quickly, though. They were deafening. Like thunderclaps. They were like the beginning of a storm. On days of electrical storms the dialogue between the beast and the field under the rain was like a pure abyss.

She called him Tiger. Any other name would have been an injustice. She told him, You Tiger, me Human.

It reached a point that the vet who took care of him refused to come back. It's dangerous, she warned her. She insisted, You are meat. You can't continue sleeping with him. At least buy yourself a weapon, she advised her.

Human said, How can you say that? The vet, who was becoming a close friend, gave her a loaded revolver the last time she went to see her. Human left it in the night stand, and forgot it was there.

Tiger and Human lived alone. Sometimes Tiger would go out strolling around the piece of land he was allowed: an area surrounded by high electric fences. The local council had imposed it as a condition for allowing Human to keep an adult tiger. Not that they'd have known what to do with the beast if they'd ordered her to give it up to them, except sacrifice it.

No one came to visit Human. Tiger was terrifying. Because of that, when Human sometimes left to go shopping, to run an errand, to the doctor, she'd leave Tiger at home, always with enough food and water to last the time she was away.

After one of those three or four day absences, Human didn't see Tiger on her return. With no sense of apprehension she entered the house, she called, Tiger, but Tiger didn't appear.

Human went up to her bedroom and there she found him, stretched out on the bed, moaning. Human didn't know that a group of wild dogs which had found a way into his field had stolen his food and he was weak.

She came over to ask him what was wrong and realised something wasn't right. She saw it in Tiger's eyes, in the throat she could see beyond his open mouth. She understood the moment her veterinarian friend had warned her about had come. Tiger stood up. He took his time. No doubt he would win. She went to the night stand and opened the drawer. Tiger bowed his head. Human realised he was asking forgiveness for what he was about to do. Human released the safety catch on the gun, held it to her temple and shot. When Tiger pounced to devour her, Human was already dead.

1

BRAVE PEOPLE DARE TO DO WHAT IS NECESSARY. FICKLE PEOPLE only dare to do what they feel like.

We fickle people don't always dare, they answer. Fear grips us. This fear, I tell them, has its root in another greater desire for something even more important to you.

Brave people dare to do what is necessary, I tell myself, I insist to myself, I repeat to myself. I must do what is right, I'm morally obliged to leave this place. That's what my mother taught me, that's what my grandmother taught me. Because we women in my family aren't Penelope, because we women in my family are Ulysses, because being Ulysses doesn't mean being a man, being Ulysses means being capable of an odyssey, even though this odyssey might not be recognised. My epic feat is to move and determine my heroism with a step perhaps small for mankind but decisive for me, a butterfly effect the consequences of which I can't even imagine.

1

THERE IS SOMETHING DECENT IN A WOUND.

In the fall of a tightrope walker, the freezing of a climber's fingers, the shot received during a revolutionary struggle, the scar left by a tricky operation, the malnutrition or dehydration as a result of a shipwreck.

I went into the pharmacy to buy toothbrushes. The pharmacist knew me. He looked at me. First in silence. Then before taking the money he asked me, How did you do that?

He was referring to the bruise on my face.

I'm so clumsy, a total disaster, I just walked into a door.

He insisted, Protocol obliges us to report it if it's anything else.

He tactfully said something else, and I realised my lie became transparent in saying I just.

There is something indecent in some wounds.

1

THERE WAS ALWAYS SOMETHING HAPPENING TO HER WHICH WAS always worse or more urgent or more important than what happened to others. Including the iguaneenie, poor iguaneenie, she never stopped doing everything to the absurd end of pleasing iguana senior.

Mama, she asked one day while we were having lunch, did I live with you or grandma as a little girl?

All of a sudden it seemed as though a typhoon had come through the window. With the same arbitrary force the iguana rose from the cushion — it was a low table, we'd eat sitting on the ground, embracing humility, she'd say, she on whom the method had no effect — and with her came the plates, the cutlery, the glasses, the bottles, the plate of lettuce, the napkins, the placemats, all swept up in that kind of cone or a cylinder ending in a point or pyramid or spiral, all mixed together, accompanied by a shout claiming to be a measured statement, How dare you ask me that? And the iguaneenie, who'd never had blood in her veins but only whatever connects zeros and ones in computers, the iguaneenie luckily kept calm and said, Because I don't know and I want to know and grandad's diary says I lived with them and grandma says so. Then the iguana suddenly disappeared and the plates, the cutlery, the glasses, the bottles, the plate of lettuce, the napkins, the placemats fell on our heads and the gale ceased and everything was destroyed, nothing was left intact, only a stillness of things forever dead.

1

IT WAS SO COMPLICATED TO MOVE TOWARDS THE WAY OUT without knowing where it was. Dragging that unusual burden. Everything would be so easy if she died. If she died. I thought it and felt relief. And feeling that relief was like easing the burden that weighed on me like a piano or an adult male lion in my arms. It was relief against my own self. A fluke.

It was not a way out.

Think of something else, something possible, something real. For example, you could kill yourself, before the tiger munches you; before the boa begins to devour you; before the scorpion sticks its stinger into you.

1

I STUDIED GEOMETRY AND ALGEBRA. I STUDIED QUANTUM PHYSICS and trigonometry. I studied philosophy and medicine. I studied everything as I sought a way to leave that coffin in which every day there was less air, less light. Lucky books, I thought. Lucky words, I thought. Lucky colours. Lucky that to open my head I'd have to cut it in half and kill myself, I thought.

Close your eyes.

Imagine yourself inside a wooden box.

Imagine the box is underground.

Now try to breathe.

1

I TRIED TO VISUALISE THE HOLE THAT SOMEONE OR SOMETHING must have made in my soul that made me mistake it for love.

Because at times I thought she loved me. That continual attention of hers, the not needing anything other than my presence. Until I realised there was no hole in me except the one she was making in my tenderest part. With admirable persistence. With a sharp-ended chisel and a hammer that sometimes hit the nail on the head and sometimes hit mine.

She made the hole in me because she needed to eat me from within. She needed to leave my shell intact so no one would suspect anything.

She was like a rat that gets inside you through the vagina.

In one of the pauses she took — her method was enter, devour, leave and pretend — she left something inside me. It was an act of carelessness. Sooner or later she had to make a mistake.

And in her error I found my strength.

1

SHARP AS A SCALPEL, IT HAD BECOME EMBEDDED IN MY FLESH and could barely be seen. I had to sink my fingers in, bloody them, to grasp the instrument for analysis. It was minuscule. So it was this — this tooth — she was using to tear me apart. That is, part of her great power lay in it. Raising it to the light it looked like a diamond. So multi-faceted.

Not even for a second did I think of using it against her. The only thing I thought about was where to hide it so she wouldn't find it.

Where would a carnivorous plant never look?

I started pondering a solution and just then she appeared. What are you doing?

1

I FEARED FOR MY LIFE. HER HANDS COVERED IN FLOUR AND EGG grew disproportionately big. Her eyes bulged out of their sockets and hung from her body, now of enormous stature, by some fine red and blue nerves that trembled as though they were threads of stars moving in the wind.

I wanted to move. Yes, I wanted to move, and I was telling myself inwardly, move, move. My feet were weighing me down, they were glued to the ground, all I could do was see her coming.

She said, Give it back to me.

Give what back? I could feel the tooth in the palm of my hand. I squeezed it until it cut me. Blood began to spread across the ground around me. The shark smiled. It kept swimming. It cleaved the water. I was within its reach.

Suddenly a squid, she hurled one of her tentacles at me and wrapped it around my neck. It was choking me. So this is asphyxia, I thought as I ran out of air. With my hands I clutched the beast's arm to free myself and the tooth fell. To retrieve it she let me go.

I was saved by the weapon with which she meant to kill me. Just before reaching a bedroom in the house to place myself beyond danger behind a locked door, she grabbed me by one of my ankles. I was about to lose my balance but twisted and gave her a hard kick with the foot that was still free. I thought I'd maybe broken her hip. I was about to worry, but logic prevailed in time and I hid in the bedroom. I placed my foot against the door. I couldn't find the key, it wasn't there, maybe she'd hidden it. The door was shaking under the plant's fists, all the floury octopus tentacles, she was screaming with carnivorous rage, and the blows half-opened the door and her eyes, on nerves as long as whips, appeared through the gap.

Sooner or later she'll get tired of it, I told myself to be able to keep holding on and stay relaxed. Stay where you are, stay this way and wait. If she catches you today, she'll kill you.

1

DID YOU EVER THINK THAT SHE WOULD KILL YOU?

Not that she would kill me, no, but it was clear that she'd leave me to die if by accident I was fatally wounded. If she was angry and I was having a heart attack, she wouldn't call an ambulance or come to my aid. No, I hadn't the least doubt about that. Her rage is as rampant as a pandemic. And it recognises no one. It grows and grows and is deaf and blind, like a gas. It has no conscience. It's a phenomenon that can only be understood through experience. It would be admirable if it wasn't horrible.

And details, of course, like occasionally ensuring that all my property was in her name. You've not modified the will you showed me, have you? You're Tom Ripley, I wanted to say. But I kept quiet. I kept quiet but called the notary to change the paperwork in secret. Surprise.

ANNULMENT

A MAN ARRIVES AT THE COUNTRY HOUSE IN WHICH HE HAS decided to live. He needs or believes he needs to be encircled by that solitude, surrounded by unthinkable wooded mountains, to develop the nanoelectricity project that will bring him wealth and glory.

He has everything under control. The material catalogued, the formula checked, optimal confidence and a serenity capable of handling any kind of mishap.

The house is on top of a hill from where the valley can be seen. The poplars, the eucalypti, the weeping willows, the rocky river and its rippling waters.

Sitting on the porch, the man inhales, filling his lungs with fresh air and as he exhales he sees an automobile crossing the gate that gives access to the property.

When it's closer he can make out that the van is familiar: that of his only friend from university. He was arriving a day before they'd agreed. They'd planned that he'd come for lunch with him: I'll give you a present, have lunch with you, see where you've holed up alone and go back to the city. That was the deal for the following day. Why had he come early?

They hug, they open a bottle of wine, with cheese and sausage to pick at. We'll get the fire going to grill the meat on the flames, what do you think? I've brought it all, wait till I go get it from the van. Want me to help you? No, no. It's not too much.

But instead of bags of meat or vegetables, instead of coal or bottles, his friend comes back with a huge cardboard box full of little holes, tied with a red bow that is moving in his hands. Have you brought a live cow?

Open it.

He opened it.

A dog.

A dog?

The man looks at his friend. The man smiles as he shakes his head.

He'll keep you company. You shouldn't be so alone.

Well, maybe it wasn't a bad idea, he'd already had one as a boy. He'd call this one Box. Because it was a boxer and had come in a box.

It was in his arms while he waved to his friend, who was still watching through the rear view mirror. When the vehicle reached the gate he raised his hand for the last time and entered the house.

Some months passed. Box and the man were making progress. The man had delved very deeply into his research. There was little left to do before showing the world the surprising results. Box had perfected the hunting of partridges, which he'd trap and then set free, as the man had shown him.

They went walking in the twilight and played football.

Then it happened. Box began to bark all day, every day. As if he hadn't known how before and was suddenly charmed by his own voice, fascinated by the increasingly strong, agile sound coming out of his body.

The man tried to quieten him, gave him a few whacks, scolded him, shouted sometimes, but nothing, nothing worked. He'd put him out of the house, but Box always came back. He didn't like being alone.

The man built a kind of chicken coop to shut him in. In a few hours one night, Box managed to destroy what had taken the man some days to put up.

I can't work like this, Box.

Box, you'll make me do what I don't want to do.

Don't provoke me, Box.

It's all your fault.

Box didn't understand. He whined, he ran around, he barked and barked.

Look, I'm a good person, I'd never resort to violence, it's you forcing me to seek alternatives that would never be part of my code of conduct.

Of course Box continued trusting the man and walking with him even though he didn't talk to him any more, even though he never patted him any more, even though they didn't play any more.

Because of that Box wasn't worried when the man approached him with a syringe and a knife. Because of that he didn't run away when he stuck the needle in and injected him with the general anaesthetic.

And so when he woke later feeling sick and couldn't bark to show his happiness at seeing his friend again, he never dreamed that man had cut his vocal cords.

1

I CAME TO BE LIKE A DECAL SOMEONE IS REMOVING LITTLE BY little by its edges, away from the surface on which it survives and gives it meaning.

1

SHE'S DEAD TO ME, SHE SAID. SHE WAS REFERRING TO HER mother. All because she'd backed her into a corner. She'd told her, You're like your father. And she'd said it in front of me. She'd been found out. Betrayed.

How could she? It's a lie, the iguana said. They all lie. My daughter, my sisters, my ex-lovers. The world is against me because I'm the bearer of a truth that unsettles them. Eat my bread and you'll recognise the essence of your spirit.

She proclaimed herself master baker. She didn't just make bread, but speeches too. She passionately underlined that manual of hers and blended its ideas to sound convincing. Follow me and I will save you.

She's dead to me, she said.

1

HOW ARE YOU? HOW HAVE YOU BEEN GETTING ON, UP TO NOW?

Are you still thinking that none of this could have happened to any of you, or are you starting to see certain parallels not with the events but with your emotions, your fears, your worries, and my situation?

When you've gone out do you feel like going home?

Would you get on the first train that passes and dream of not returning and that absence having no repercussions?

Flight with no consequences or reprisals.

So what?

What do you think?

And being without him.

And being without her.

Without them, even.

Without the carnivorous plants devouring you and making you feel that this isn't living.

What is living?

Let's define it in five words.

One. Two. Three. Four. Five.

Why not these ones?

1

FOR THE FIRST TIME IN MY LIFE I SPENT THE WHOLE DAY LYING. A painful division between reality and fiction. I put on an all-round, non-existent happiness. It was like being the living dead. Like being a memory, an invention, a story. A speech. There was no overlap between what I thought, what I said, and what I did. I wasn't, any more. I was nothing. I'd lost my freedom. The hunter had hit the lion on the head. The fish was in the net. The beast deep within the carnivore. It was now or never. I had to understand there was no other solution.

1

THREE CACHES OF SUPPLIES. THREE PLACES THAT MUST BE reached. Deliver all three caches to all three places without crossing a single line.

Admit it. There are things which are impossible.
The carnivorous plant would never harmlessly flower.

WHOEVER HAS GONE THROUGH SOMETHING SIMILAR AND THINKS my situation is worse than theirs, pay attention. What they are doing is justifying their predator and is the reason they are still in touch and believe that they're friends. The psychologist made it very clear, you can't be her friend, you'll continue feeling like her prey, they always need one, they can't be without. It might be her mother, daughter, or the holy spirit. But something, someone.

Whoever thinks that my case is worse than theirs perhaps tells themselves, a carnivorous plant is worse than a raccoon, a plant is worse than a fish, a stem than a vine, a scorpion than a rattlesnake.

Warning.

Watch out.

Danger.

Stay alert for signs.

1

ONE DAY I FORGOT TO TIE MYSELF TO THE LIFELINE, THE proverbial metallic thread that prevents a storm from pulling you from the boat. The wind was howling. I was trying to tie a reef knot. Without help from her. Every manoeuvre was without help from her. I don't understand sailboats, said the plant.

I fell into the water. It was freezing. The waves were high.

I weighed so much. I weighed a lot. Clothed in an overcoat, boots. All multiplied by water and salt.

Desperately I hooked myself onto the ladder just in time. My body was a solid mountain unavoidably sinking in the sea. She poked her head overboard. She looked around. She disappeared. She didn't know how to navigate the boat. She didn't have a clue.

I was about to give up. But in a mad impulse of survival I put a foot on the lower rung of the folded ladder. I didn't have time to ask her to release it and besides, I suspected she wouldn't do it.

I pushed myself upwards. I'd done it. I brought the boat to and entered the cabin, where she was sitting to shelter from the rain, to find clothes to change into.

With a high fever for the following week, I kept feeling that if I'd died she would have been adrift. That image was etched on my memory. It was a premonition. A message that had to be read and obeyed.

The only thing she said to me was, I thought that you knew how to sail, I'm never coming out to sea with you again.

1

THE FINAL PIECE OF MADNESS I ENDURED WAS ON A GREEK island. I'd invited her to spend a few days there before opening a solo exhibition in Athens. Some stone sculptures I'd done over the previous two years. For me exhibiting sculpture in Greece was like building a dome in Florence. I don't know if you understand.

We were on a deserted beach. Turquoise waters. Fine, clean, dazzling white sand. A few gulls. Her luscious skin. The sound of the sea. Mouths and kisses. Paradise.

Her snake of rage was stalking us. As usual, I didn't see it coming. It appeared in the form of a question.

Apparently before leaving home Ibana had taken the trouble of revising the thousands of books in my library. All the first pages. Dedications from the past, if there were any.

Who is Emma?

I shook my head.

What are you denying? Who is Emma?

I knew there was no right answer, so I shook my head again as if that attitude of silence could magically uncover a solution, a way of making that Eden last.

We were naked. She got dressed. With a fearful carefulness I didn't recognise. She aimed a kick at me. I pulled away in time.

She disappeared. For four days. I asked everyone, everywhere. It was as though the earth had swallowed her up. I should have gone to Athens on my own. To the opening of the exhibition on my own.

I couldn't report it to the police because she was an adult. I suspected that it was another one of her acts of torture. I couldn't be sure.

Anguish is a thing that eats you alive. You see the pieces of yourself, yet don't have the strength to put them back together. You can only observe your own decomposition, your quartering.

Finally she answered her mobile. On the fifth day. And what did I do? I asked for forgiveness because her madness pained me. I just wanted to go and get her, to take her to a safe place. I couldn't sink any lower.

What had been broken was absolute.

1

SHE WAS WRITING OUR NAMES IN CHALK TO THE WORLD AND rubbing out mine. That's how you'll learn. That was the phrase she used. She said it just like that. That's how you'll learn.

Was it she who had to teach me?

Oh, how much I learned.

Thank you, teacher.

HUMILIATION

THE QUEUE WAS LONG. SHE WAS IMPATIENT. THE FLIGHT HAD been tedious and turbulent. She'd slept very little. She'd spent most of the time going over her notes for the conference. She'd found a couple of drawings by her daughters among the papers. So sweet. They told her they'd miss her a lot. The littlest one had drawn the cakes their grandmother made, in case you get hungry, and the other a map of the world on which she'd painted her country and the country she was going to in red, so you don't get lost.

How long 'til you get back? the little one had asked her when they went to the airport to say goodbye.

Seven days.

That's a long time.

Well, a week.

She smiled. That seemed more acceptable to her. The big girl acted as if it was all the same to her, and told the little one, Mummy is going for work, don't worry, she'll call us every day on the phone, won't you? And she looked at her, willing her to confirm it.

Every day.

It had been complicated to get the visa. Rich countries were armouring their borders. Who wants a pauper at their table?

The queue moved forward in dribs and drabs. When there were three people ahead of her to reach the police officer in charge of passport control, she got all the necessary documents ready: her credit cards, the travel and medical insurance, a good quantity of money, the invitation from the university, the letter from friends, the visa, the vaccination record and, even though they didn't ask for it, a medical report.

Her turn. The agent looked at her severely. Perhaps annoyed by her brightly coloured clothing or the colour of her skin, or by her dignified, calm appearance, the lack of fear. Perhaps that's what was happening to the policeman, he felt challenged by her showing him no deference.

He grabbed the passport and all the papers she provided. He started to examine them on the counter. She lost sight of them. Minutes later he said, The medical report is missing.

She said, It's with the others I've given you, but it wasn't even a requirement for entry. I brought it just in case.

He didn't let her continue. He'd already raised his arm, called another agent, a tall blonde woman, in an impeccable navy uniform.

Come with me.

It was cold, or so it seemed, in the inhospitable room — a steel table, dirty white walls, no chair — where they asked her to undress. Unperturbed, they watched her. The official who had accompanied her remained by the door. The other put on latex gloves without looking away from her, from her and the clothes she was dropping on the ground.

When they asked her to place her hands on the back of her neck and her head on the desk so they could probe inside her, she closed her eyes and thought of her daughters' drawings, their grandmother's cakes, the hunger for so many things, and the maps of the world, the pain of so many others. The cool steel against her forehead reminded her that this was real and she was alive.

1

WHAT CAN BE DONE SO SOMEONE YOU LOVE SO MUCH WILL believe in your love?

I'd filled social media with romantic statements. I'd let her know. I'd drawn her. Painted her. Sculpted her. I'd dedicated paintings to her. People believed in her. I'd given her a place not written in chalk, one that couldn't be erased. The place from which she betrayed my trust and my respect.

The slander ends here and now, Ibana.

It ends today.

1

IT'S A BLOW TO THE HEAD. FROM WITHIN. IN THE BLINK OF AN eye. And you see it. You see yourself there. The paintbrushes help you. Your past helps you. You have a life. You've always had it.

The way out of the labyrinth was overhead. A change of perspective was required. You need to pile all your things like a ladder to get up there and abandon them afterwards. You have to leave everything behind. Let go.

You decide. You can do this.

I'm going. There's nothing I won't believe. I won't invest my life in convincing her that love exists and isn't a title deed.

No time left.

It's over.

I had to break some of the filaments blocking the way out.

1

THE STRATEGY.

One: Breathe clean air, from outside the plant. Fill your lungs. Oxygenate them. Observe the recovery of brain capacity.

Two: Tell someone what has happened.

Three: Don't go back under any circumstances.

Four: Remember who you were before being hunted by the plant.

Five: Observe other victims from a distance and identify what you have in common.

Six: Calculate the impact of the fall.

Seven: Know that nothing could be worse than being trapped by the carnivore.

Eight: Keep your heart up.

Nine: Jump.

1

A JUMP CAN LOOK LIKE A FALL FOR THE WHOLE TIME THE JUMP lasts.

But a jump is a jump.

And a fall is a fall.

The jump is chosen.

The fall is endured.

1

THERE IS NOTHING MORE DANGEROUS TO THE ONE WHO HAS been prey than the space they leave in the plant. It has its shape and a centrifugal force takes action, attracting all that is close by. When it recognises the mould it traps the prey once more.

There is a delicate but very powerful web between the plant and its food.

She phoned me after a few days.

Since you say I never apologise, I'm calling to apologise. She said it in the tone of a plant open-mouthed at its garden of one-person delights.

The mobile was burning me. At first I shook my head, no. Then my voice. No, Ibana. No.

To me that No was like a surfboard with which to frighten away the hungriest of sharks. I was on the verge of approaching her to pull out a tooth like a trophy, but no. The trophy was getting out of there.

1

THE PLANT DEVELOPED AN UNUSUAL RASH.

She accused me of having provoked it.

She got attention and pity from the Bread & Circus customers. She showed it off.

You'll learn from it. You'll learn. That's what she said.

And chewed-up me there, watching her from afar, asking the lawyers — the ones she chose — to cut that indissoluble bond, even if they made the cut close to the root and the wound was left on my terrain.

Cut, cut.

1

AROUND THEN, A FRIEND FROM THE PAST I'D NOT SEEN IN A LONG time called me. She was having some problems and asked for my help. Of course, of course, I told her. Whatever it takes.

I supported her in her worries and afterwards we chatted and I told her everything. She was horrified and crossed herself and expressed her repulsion and condemnation of the carnivorous beast.

1

THE WOMAN WHO HAD CALLED TO ASK FOR A FAVOUR HAD a notion that perhaps you too embrace. You must have done something, Andrea, nothing like that would ever happen to me.

She got close to the plant to prove her theory.

And the plant swallowed her.

1

IT WAS CLEAR THE PLANT WOULDN'T STOP BEING A DANGER TO me until she obtained another piece of flesh to satisfy her. The traitor. Done.

It took me months to spit out all the loathing I'd vomited within.

You'll ask what remains after that imprisonment. What remains when you get out.

Freedom remains. Abundant freedom. The elephant's, the lion's.

LIBERATION

THE PRECIPICE IS SHAKY. IT CAN BE GLIMPSED JUTTING OUT AT the end of the slope.

She starts to run. Faster and faster. Her head wants her to brake. Her heart gives her courage.

When her feet reach the edge, the abyss claims her and sucks her down a few metres. Her head intervenes: See?

Her heart responds and opens the wings that allow a sudden swoop upwards, outwards.

This is flying.

ANDREA MAYO

The question is ... who is Andrea Mayo? We find her origin in the short story *La Carta Perdida De Andrea Mayo* (The Lost Letter of Andrea Mayo), by the Argentinian-Catalan author Flavia Company, who brought Andrea to life by turning her into one of her heteronyms.

Andrea is a strong, confident, daring woman. A woman who merges with literature, who speaks to us from the other side of the mirror, someone who, out of fiction, brings us reality. She, like other characters from Flavia Company's imaginary world, has come to eliminate labels and break frontiers. She becomes part of whoever reads her.

As her creator always says, in her books fiction is on the cover and the reality is inside.

LAURA MCGLOUGHLIN HAS BEEN A FREELANCE TRANSLATOR FROM Catalan and Spanish since completing a Masters in literary translation at the University of East Anglia. She was awarded the inaugural British Centre for Literary Translation Catalan-English Translation Mentorship in 2011. Among others she has translated work by Llüisa Cunillé, Maria Barbal, Flavia Company, Toni Hill Gumbao, and Joan Brossa, as well as for director Carlos Saura, the Museu d'Art Contemporani de Barcelona and the Association of Writers in Catalan (AELC). Her most recent translations are *Wilder Winds*, a collection of short stories by Bel Olid and the non-fiction essay *Hairless*, also by Bel Olid. She was Translator in Residence at the British Centre for Literary Translation during spring 2022.

annapont

We translate female authors who write in minority languages. Only women. Only minority languages. This is our choice.

We know that we only win if we all win, that's why we are proud to be fair trade publishers. And we are committed to supporting organisations in the UK that help women to live freely and with dignity.

We are 3TimesRebel.